Praise for
MURDER IN VOLUME

"Keeps the reader intrigued. More, more!"
—Charlaine Harris,
author of *A Fool and His Money*

"Clever, compelling, original, and chock-full of detection lore. *Murder in Volume* is like finding a mint Christie hidden in your great-aunt's tea cosy."
—Carolyn Hart,
author of *Death on Demand* and the Henrie O mysteries

"How ideal to play sleuth in the company of two such appealing and intriguing characters as Megan Clark and Ryan Stevens—especially when their 'Dr. Watsons' include an eccentric hodge-podge of mystery fans. A great beginning for an exciting new series."
—Joan Lowery Nixon,
author of the Thumbprint Mysteries
and past president of Mystery Writers of America

"Wonderfully clever role reversals, a plethora of plot puzzles, an intriguing point of view technique, and an amazingly well-read author of mysteries old and new make this new series by veteran mystery writer D. R. Meredith a delight for mystery lovers of all stripes."
—Marlys Millhiser,
author of *Nobody Dies in a Casino*

continued on next page . . .

MURDER
PAST DUE

D. R. MEREDITH

BERKLEY PRIME CRIME, NEW YORK

MURDER PAST DUE

A Berkley Prime Crime Book / published by arrangement with the author

PRINTING HISTORY
Berkley Prime Crime edition / March 2001

The Penguin Putnam Inc. World Wide Web site address is http://www.penguinputnam.com

ISBN: 0-425-17800-5

Berkley Prime Crime Books are published by The Berkley Publishing Group, a division of Penguin Putnam Inc., 375 Hudson Street, New York, New York 10014.
The name BERKLEY PRIME CRIME and the BERKLEY PRIME CRIME design are trademarks belonging to Penguin Putnam Inc.

PRINTED IN THE UNITED STATES OF AMERICA

10 9 8 7 6 5 4 3 2 1

With the exception of the Gorman murder, all other murders described are actual cases. The body was real, the blood was real, the verdict a matter of public record. Otherwise, any resemblance between my characters and any persons actually living in Amarillo, Texas, is coincidental and utterly unintentional. The events portrayed are a figment of my imagination and not meant to mirror actual events, past or present.

D. R. MEREDITH

*Here's to all the gals in Medical Records
who wanted me to write a book for them.*

*Connie, Elaine, Martha, Sara, Twoie, Arlene,
Melinda, Bennie, the two Nancys, Melissa, Renee,
Emily, Josie, and Dana, this one is for you.*

ACKNOWLEDGMENTS

To my husband, Mike, who spent so many hours grubbing in courthouse records for details on old murders. Nobody could have been so helpful to a desperate writer trying to make her deadline. Mike, I love you. And a heartfelt thank you to Mary Kate Tripp, retired journalist and friend, who patiently answered questions and verified information on Amarillo's most scandalous murder cases. If I made mistakes, it is my own fault and not that of those who assisted me.

PROLOGUE

"We never give up on an unsolved murder, and that includes the Gorman case. No one was ever formally charged, so as far as we're concerned, it's still an open case, even if it is twenty years old."

LIEUTENANT JERRY CARR
on Amarillo's unsolved crimes,
Amarillo Globe-News, September 9

The first Mrs. Gorman, the frail city girl from Back East—as any locale farther away than Missouri was inevitably referred to—prevailed upon the whipcord-lean, leathery-faced rancher to build her a gazebo, a Victorian lacework of oak painted the most brilliant white, with benches lining its circular walls, and bright yellow cushions to sit on. Her husband muttered about how the gazebo wouldn't look much like the house, but the first Mrs. Gorman shuddered to think of her retreat built of limestone blocks, cold and hard and quarried by prisoners from the hills around Austin. She could not bear it. She felt she could not survive if she did not have her gazebo, light and airy and tucked away in the grove of cottonwood trees her husband planted when he first set foot upon this land and dreamed of a mansion to match him. She didn't begrudge him his limestone mansion, but she felt oppressed by all that weight of stone, much as she felt oppressed by all the open space that stretched from horizon to horizon and as high as one could see. She was not suited for the high plains of Texas but for small, cozy places. She wanted her gazebo, even though the wind blew fiercely through its open latticework most of the time, and the snow drifted higher than its roof in the winter. But come spring and summer, she would lie about on her yellow cushions, and when her body quickened with her first child, it was in her gazebo that she waited out her time. It was to the gazebo that she took her infant son, refusing the help of the nurse, and sang to him of far-off shores she knew she would never live to see. It was to the gazebo she fled when she could no longer conceal the coughing spasms that left her lace-trimmed handkerchiefs speckled with blood. It was in the gazebo that her husband found her, lying gracefully upon her yellow cushions, clutching a blood-soaked handkerchief, her pale skin already cool to the touch.

There was a second Mrs. Gorman, a sturdy woman to match the limestone mansion. The rancher boarded up the gazebo and never spoke of his first wife again. Never was he seen to smile so freely again, and he never laughed.

But that was then, thought the newest Mrs. Gorman, wife of the owner's grandson, the owner whose mother died in the gazebo of consumption, as tuberculosis was called in those days. And this was now, and her husband's grandfather restored the gazebo to its lacy beauty and ordered new yellow cushions for its benches. She leaned back, crossing her ankles in that obligatory ladylike way her mother-in-law insisted upon, and listened to the cottonwood trees sing in the evening breeze. Grandfather Gorman said only the cottonwood tree truly sang. Their leaves rustled in a melody so beautiful even the newest Mrs. Gorman appreciated it, and she was not into soft music. Punk was more her style, but she supposed she would have to learn to endure classical music. After all, the Gormans always attended the symphony, and so far as she knew, the Amarillo symphony didn't play punk. Marrying into money did have its drawbacks. One had to appreciate Culture with a capital C, and her background was lacking in what the Gormans considered culture. But it didn't matter. She was Mrs. Gorman, and she was going to learn to be good at it. But first this meeting. Surely he would understand that the rules had changed. She could not be what she was.

She rose to pace the twelve feet from one side of the gazebo to another, then sat down next to its arched entrance and spread the skirt of her white robe about her. She supposed she should have changed, but the summons came so unexpectedly that she didn't have time. It wasn't as if she wasn't decently dressed. The robe was satin, but it was buttoned to her throat and the belt tied. He wouldn't get any ideas that she was trying to tempt him. That was over. No, this was about setting the ground rules for the rest of their lives. They could hardly go on the way they had been. It was about decorum. Even someone with her working class background knew about decorum. It was about behavior and how to treat one another, and she would not be treated the way she had been. She was a Gorman wife now, and there were certain rules about how a Gorman wife was treated.

She rubbed her arms as a sudden chill made her shiver—but not from fear. She wasn't afraid of him. He danced to her tune, not the other way around.

She started at a soft sound, and then he was there, his eyes blazing at her in the moonlight. In one hand he held a pool cue, but she couldn't ask him why, not when his lips were drawn back like a snarling dog. She didn't mean to make him so angry, she really didn't, and when he grabbed her arm, she tried to pull away. The satin, the satin she so loved to touch was stronger than she supposed and would not rip or give way to free her. Her last conscious thought was that she wished she had worn a lacy blouse. Lace always tore so easily.

The rest of the family found her husband sitting on the steps of the gazebo while she lay on the floor just inside. He had put a yellow cushion under her head. "So she will be comfortable," he said. When the police came, he was still sitting there, holding the pool cue he said he found by her body.

1

"Who is that citizen?"
"That's my next-door neighbor."
"He looks as though his mind could stand a little laundering."

JOHN McGUIRE
(reporter Michael Ward) and a bit player,
Stranger on the Third Floor, 1940

"I have a suggestion," said Megan Clark, scooting to the very edge of the couch.

The seating for Murder by the Yard Reading Circle consisted of a couch, two upholstered chairs, and five or more folding chairs, depending on whether the regular members brought guests. Megan and Ryan always sat on the couch, since Ryan insisted he had spent too many hours of his life at too many faculty meetings sitting in uncomfortable auditorium seats, and he had no intention of further punishing his behind by sitting on a folding chair on his own time. Megan supposed he had a point, but she suspected his insistence on sitting on the couch had as much to do with having a comfortable seat in which to doze during the meetings of Murder by the Yard as it did with his wish to avoid folding chairs. Couches had arms on which to prop your elbow, which in turn allowed you to prop your chin in the palm of your hand, scoot back into the corner of the couch, open the evening's selection on your lap, lower your head as though reading, and as long as you didn't snore, everyone would think you were just extraordinarily quiet and attentive to others' comments. You couldn't do that in a folding chair, although Ryan had tried sleeping sitting bolt upright. He slipped off the side of the chair, fell against the corner of a briefcase belonging to Herbert, "Call Me Herb," Jackson III, and blacked his eye. The Twins, unrelated but nearly identical white-haired elderly ladies named Rosemary Pittman and Lorene Getz, thought Ryan had suffered a "spell," a nonspecific word used by their generation to mean anything from epilepsy to a stroke to simple dizziness. It could also mean a variety of mental illnesses, but Megan didn't think the Twins thought Ryan was mental.

"What's your suggestion, Megan?" asked Agnes Caldwell, owner of Time and Again Bookstore, where Murder by the Yard met each week.

Megan laced her fingers together to keep from talking with her hands, which she frequently did, especially when she was excited. Not that there was anything wrong with using hand gestures when carrying on a conversation, but when you're only a little over five feet tall and have curly red hair and are cursed with being called cute, then you want to act as sophisticated and dignified as possible to counteract the cute factor. Otherwise, people tend to treat you like a twelve-year-old instead of a serious scholar who earned a Ph.D. by the time she was twenty-five. In her next reincarnation, if there was such a thing, Megan planned on being at least six inches taller. Short people never got any respect.

"Since this month will mark our six-month anniversary as a reading club specializing in mysteries, I thought we might celebrate by touring the famous murder sites in Amarillo," said Megan. "We could pass out press releases to the newspaper and TV and radio stations. Maybe one of them would mention the tour on air, and we might recruit some new members."

"I think that's a wonderful idea, Megan," said Agnes. "It surely would attract new members—and new customers, which I can always use. And between us, I'm sure we can think of enough of Amarillo's famous murder cases to make the tour interesting."

"You mean murder sites like the Tex Thornton case?" asked Rosemary Pittman, the wealthy member of the Twins. "I remember my mother talking about that case in whispers so my younger sister and I wouldn't hear any of the details. You have to understand that my mother was of the generation and social class that never mentioned the word *sex* out loud. Of course, my sister and I just sneaked the newspaper into my room and read all about it. I can remember how indignant I was at my mother's attitude. It was the summer before my senior year at Southern Methodist University, and I thought I knew all about the birds and the bees. Of course, compared to today's middle school student, I was terribly naive. I think it was better that way, don't you, Lorene?"

Lorene Getz, the other member of the Twins, nodded her head. "Girls were protected in our day."

Megan didn't comment. She opposed keeping young girls in ignorance, be it sexual or economic, but she liked the Twins too much to argue with them. Personally, she couldn't imagine her own mother keeping her ignorant of any fact of life. Her mother believed in full disclosure, but what else could one expect of a woman who carried magic markers, wooden stakes, and poster board in the trunk of her car just in case she needed to make a picket sign for or against some cause at short notice?

"If you want a case with sex in it, how about the L. R. Wynn case?" asked Randal Anderson, professor of English at Amarillo College, and self-professed expert on symbolism in mysteries. Most of the time Megan considered him as irritating as a kernel of popcorn caught between her teeth.

"Wynn shot his wife's lover at noon on Fillmore Street in front of the First National Bank in downtown Amarillo in front of dozens of witnesses," continued Randal. "I was a teenager when that case happened, but I remember it. That was the scandal of the century, because the lover was a well-known oilman."

"No, it wasn't," said Ryan Stevens, straightening up and closing the book on his lap.

"Wasn't what, Ryan?" asked Megan, surprised that he was awake. She usually had to elbow him out of a sound sleep at the end of a meeting, unless the book discussed was by Arthur Conan Doyle, Poe, or Sue Grafton. Doyle and Poe were on his college reading list, and he had actually read *A is for Alibi*. He said the character reminded him of her. Megan couldn't see the resemblance herself.

"The scandal of the century. The Wynn case wasn't the scandal of the century. The Boyce-Sneed feud was."

"I forgot about that one," said Randal, smoothing his goatee. "My grandfather used to talk about the Boyces and the Sneeds. He was a Sneed man, even though he thought Beal Sneed stepped out of bounds a little bit."

"He stepped out more than a little bit," said Agnes Caldwell, sounding indignant. "My mother was on the Boyce side, and she had nothing good to say about Beal Sneed. You know, Randal, not very long ago, you and I would not be in the same club together. In fact, I wouldn't even serve you if you came in the store. I re-

member my mother turning down dinner invitations if
the Sneeds had also been invited. Of course, any hostess
with any knowledge of the social scene would never
invite both sides of the feud to the same party. If you
were a Boyce supporter, you were not friends with the
Sneed supporters."

"A feud! How fascinating from the standpoint of anthropology," said Megan, wrinkling her forehead in
thought. "I'm sure I can find one of my professional
journals that would accept an article on a twentieth century feud if I approach the subject carefully. I mean, I
couldn't make it sound too Hatfield and McCoy, or my
article would be turned down. Professional journals expect a certain level of scholarship. I would have to tie
it into the culture in general, of which the feud is a
radical representation of cultural mores."

"There's nothing particularly unique to Panhandle culture about a man shooting his wife's lover," objected
Ryan. "Historically speaking, it's probably happened a
million times during mankind's march to no-fault divorce."

"I'm sure it has," agreed Megan. "But we're talking
about a murder triggering a *family* feud in the twentieth
century in the United States, between families of the
same social class, where literally you had to check over
your guest list to make sure feuding members and their
supporters were not invited to the same party."

"Now we sue for wrongful death," said Herbert, "Call
Me Herb," Jackson III, tugging on his vest. Herb believed in wearing the lawyer uniform of three-piece suits
and a discreet tie to all functions, be it a formal dinner
or a casual meeting of Murder by the Yard.

"Exactly!" exclaimed Megan. "Like the Goldbergs
and the Browns sued OJ. In today's society, harsh feel-

ings over criminal actions are formalized and legalized and politicized. We don't see hostesses writing out their guest list and checking it twice anymore."

"I don't know about that," said Ryan. "I can't imagine OJ and the Goldbergs being invited to the same dinner party."

"You're missing the point, Ryan," said Megan. "We're talking about Amarillo's upper crust, which doesn't amount to that many families. When was this feud, anyway?"

"Nineteen-twelve," said Ryan.

"Nineteen-twelve! But Agnes, I thought you said your mother turned down dinner invitations if the other family was invited, but surely your mother wasn't even born or was a very small child," said Megan.

Agnes nodded. "Mother was born in 1915, but you have to realize, Megan, that feuds are handed down from generation to generation, like the family silver. This one finally petered out in the late 1940s or early 1950s."

"That's right," said Rosemary. "My grandmother defied my grandfather and attended the hearing after Beal Sneed shot Al Boyce, Jr. It was the first time she had ever been in the courthouse, since women weren't allowed to vote or sit on juries. She felt so sorry for Mrs. Boyce, Sr., and Lena Sneed, even though she disapproved of Lena's behavior. No one of that generation wanted their dirty linen washed in public, and nothing was more public than that hearing."

"Did your grandmother attend the trial, too, Rosemary?" asked Megan, pulling a notebook out of her backpack and finding a fresh page. She might as well take notes now while everyone was in a mood to talk.

"She couldn't," said Ryan. "The trial was held in Vernon on a change of venue. Sneed was acquitted despite the circumstances. Defense of the home, you know. Justifiable homicide."

"You seem to know a lot about the case, Ryan," said Megan.

"Sneed's first victim was Colonel A. G. Boyce, who happened to have been the manager of the XIT Ranch from 1888 to 1905. That's the only reason I know about the feud. The whole sordid affair is part of ranching history in this area, and ranching history is one of my particular interests."

"His *first* victim?" asked Megan. "Who was his second victim?"

"Al Boyce, Jr., his wife's lover," replied Ryan.

"Then who was Colonel A. G. Boyce?"

"Al Boyce, Jr.'s father."

"My God! The father and the son?" asked Megan.

"It's an ugly part of Panhandle history," said Ryan, shrugging his shoulders.

"At least only men were killed in that case. What about the A. D. Payne case?" asked Call Me Herb, the reading circle's would-be John Grisham. "My grandfather was the first policeman at the crime scene, and he used to talk about the case after I decided to go to law school. He wanted to make sure that I would never defend a man who killed his wife. "Poor little Mrs. Payne," he used to say. "She never knew she was living with a monster."

"I've heard about the Payne case," said Ryan, "but it doesn't compare to the Boyce-Sneed feud."

"Tell us why, Ryan," said Megan, her ballpoint poised to take more notes and hoping Ryan didn't suddenly decide that talking about real murder was a bad influence on the membership, meaning her. Even though he wouldn't admit it, he still thought that her finding two murder victims was somehow linked to Murder by the Yard and the whole milieu of reading and discussing mysteries. That wasn't true at all—at least, not completely true. The first murder would have occurred whether she had been a member or not. The second murder was a little iffy. If she had not talked Murder by the Yard into sponsoring a string figure convention, then the second murder wouldn't have happened, or rather, it wouldn't have happened at her convention. But it would have happened. Megan was convinced of that.

Ryan stared at the ceiling, and Megan knew she was safe. Ryan always stared at the ceiling whenever he was preparing to lecture, whether to his college classes or to her. She slowly released the breath she had been holding when he lowered his head and eased to the front of the couch in case he might want to pace. She quietly turned to a clean page in her notebook and sat with pen poised and breath held.

"In October 1911, Lena Sneed, Beal Sneed's wife, took her husband's hand and led him outside to a porch swing, and admitted that she had been having an affair with Al Boyce, Jr. That's the scenario, according to Sneed's testimony at his trial. Also according to his testimony, he had no inkling that his wife was unfaithful, even though allegedly the whole town knew what was going on, from the telephone operators to the servants to all the neighbors. The old homily says the wife, or in this case, husband, is the last to know, and maybe Beal Sneed really didn't know. Or maybe he did and intimidated his wife into confessing, although I never heard that Lena was spineless enough to be intimidated into much of anything. Maybe she really did admit she loved Al Boyce, Jr., and maybe she really did say they were going to South America to start a new life. Maybe that's the way it happened, but in view of his subsequent actions, I think Sneed may have confronted her," said Ryan, sitting comfortably on the edge of the couch with forearms resting on his thighs and his hands clasped together.

"You must mean because he imprisoned her so quickly after her alleged confession?" asked Agnes.

"What!" said Megan in a tone of voice she instantly regretted. It was almost a yelp, and whenever she yelped, Ryan always thought she was becoming far too emotionally involved in whatever she was doing to the detriment of the peace and well-being of the community. His words, not hers. Personally, she thought his reactions were exaggerated.

"Sneed committed his wife to Arlington Heights Sanitarium in Fort Worth," continued Ryan, but with a sharp look at Megan. "For moral insanity."

"I told you," said Agnes. "He locked her up."

Megan took a deep breath to control her indignation— or rather her expression of it. She mustn't yelp. "You mean this man locked up his own wife in some prison? And for *moral insanity!* That's—that's obscene!"

"That's a bit of a harsh judgment," said Randal. "He may have wanted to give her time to think on her actions and whether she really was infatuated with Al Boyce, Jr. And the sanitarium wasn't a prison. I imagine it was a mighty fancy place for the time."

"A rose by any other name, Randal," said Megan. "I bet you all the rooms had locks on the outside of the doors, and I'll further bet you that the staff was watching every breath Mrs. Sneed took. That's awful!"

Ryan gave her another sharp look, and she quickly started making notes. "At any rate, it's a moot point," said Ryan, "because Al Boyce, Jr., rescued her, and the two fled to Canada."

"Good for Al Boyce, Jr.!" exclaimed Megan, raising a clenched fist.

"Not exactly. Beal Sneed hired the Pinkertons, although according to my source, he was the one who actually tracked them down and had them arrested in Winnipeg, Canada."

"On what charges?" asked Megan. "Surely it wasn't illegal to travel with someone who wasn't your wife. It might be immoral, but I don't see how it was illegal."

"You're the anthropologist, Megan," said Ryan. "You're the one who is always talking about interpreting actions according to the beliefs of the time."

Megan flinched. She was always preaching that—and it was true—but somehow this was different. Maybe because it happened in her town, even though she hadn't been born for another sixty-plus years.

"I'm sorry I interrupted, Ryan, and you're right, of course. Please go on."

He looked at her as though he didn't quite trust her apology. "At any rate, Lena was released into the custody of her husband and her father, who was Tom Synder of Clayton, New Mexico, another pioneer rancher and a good friend of Beal Sneed."

"She must have felt horrible," said Candi Hobbs, a graduate student working on a thesis on crime fiction, and the significant other of Randal Anderson. "I can imagine how I would feel if the police arrested Randal and me and my father came to pick me up. I don't know about Mrs. Sneed's father, but mine would lecture me all the way home. And think how long it took in those days to get from Winnipeg to Clayton, New Mexico."

"If her father was anything like my father, she would

have wished she had jumped off a cliff rather than listen to him preach at her," said Lorene Getz. "My father was a good man, but he had strict notions of right and wrong. If he had preached at me all the way from Canada, I would have confessed to armed robbery and triple murder just to shut him up."

Rosemary patted her friend's hand. "My father didn't preach at us girls—he left that to Mother—but he had a look that could make me feel absolutely unworthy. I can't imagine riding all the way from Canada with my father giving me That Look. If I was a young woman in that age, I would have locked myself in the bathroom."

"She wasn't all that young," said Randal. "She and Sneed had been married for twelve years before she decided she had made a mistake in choosing Sneed over Boyce."

"What do you mean, choosing Sneed over Boyce?" asked Candi. "You mean in meekly allowing herself to be marched onto the train by her father and husband?" Megan looked at Candi in surprise. This was the first time she had ever heard shy little Candi sound indignant.

"No, Candi," said Ryan. "Sneed and Boyce and Lena grew up together in Georgetown, outside of Austin, and both men courted her when they all went to school at Southwestern University in Georgetown. She chose Sneed and was apparently satisfied with her choice for twelve years. From an objective point of view, one could say that Sneed had some justification in believing that Boyce was responsible for alienating his wife's affections."

"I don't remember, Ryan," said Agnes. "Which side of the feud was your family on?"

Megan thought Ryan looked uncomfortable, as if he

suddenly had a gas bubble. "From what I've been able to learn, my grandparents tried to stay neutral like everybody did, but of course that was impossible. The town was too small, the social strata too thin, and inevitably everyone began to choose sides, even if they didn't want to. My family was made up of pioneer ranchers, and I guess you'd call them members of the so-called upper crust, so when they were forced to take a side, they were Sneed supporters. That's not to say that they approved of Beal Sneed's behavior—they did not—but the fact that Lena Sneed had apparently been happy for twelve years sort of stuck in my grandfather's craw. He always thought that Beal and Lena would have stayed the course without any trouble if Boyce hadn't stuck his nose in their marital business, and I think my grandfather had a logical argument. I tend to agree with him."

"Your grandfather didn't know that, and you can't either, Ryan," said Agnes, a frown of disapproval on her face.

Ryan shook his head. "No, I don't, but I think that Lena would have slipped the traces a lot earlier than twelve years after the wedding if she had been that unhappy. She knew Boyce, he was a former beau of hers as well as Beal Sneed's friend. He was always in town while Sneed was frequently traveling on business. Boyce was good looking and charming and probably flirted with his old girlfriend, and the flirtation led to seduction. The charm of the forbidden fruit led her into an affair she might not have carried on if circumstances had been different."

"Slipped the traces? The charm of the forbidden fruit? Ryan, you're speaking in frontier Victorian," said Megan. "The fact is the man—Sneed—locked up his wife in an insane asylum. Peter, Peter, pumpkin eater, had a wife and couldn't keep her. Locked her in a pumpkin shell and there he kept her very well. I guess Peter's wife didn't have a man who loved her enough to rescue her. Lena Sneed was luckier."

Ryan's eyebrows drew together in a frown. "The fact is that we don't know enough about the relationship between Boyce and Lena or between Lena and Beal Sneed to make judgments—and Lena did go back to her husband."

"Before or after he shot Boyce?" asked Megan.

"Before. I can't tell you the exact date without checking court records, except it was probably in late January or early February of 1912, after he shot Colonel A. G. Boyce, Sr., because he and Lena lived in a Dallas boardinghouse for several months afterward."

Megan shook her head in disbelief. "I can't imagine her going back."

"Of course, you can't, Megan. You're too young, isn't she, Rosemary?" said Lorene.

"Much too young," agreed Rosemary. "Megan, dear, you're an independent woman who can support yourself, but what could Lena do? How would she make a living? Who would hire her? The infamous adulteress? Should she live with her father the rest of her life? Listen to his reproaches, and I'm fairly certain he reproached her, or she wouldn't have returned to Beal Sneed. And just imagine what that must have been like. As angry as Beal Sneed was, Lena would have had to grovel, beg his forgiveness, but forever after, the affair was between them like an unwelcome guest at dinner."

"And something else," said Call Me Herb. "Divorce was a shameful alternative, and besides, no-fault divorce wasn't available in Texas until 1973. If Beal Sneed hadn't wanted a divorce even though Lena did, it wouldn't have been granted."

"She was trapped then, wasn't she?" asked Megan.

"She didn't have to have an affair with Boyce," said Randal. "If she had wanted him, she should have married him instead of Sneed. Once she made her choice, she should have stood by Sneed."

"So we go from frontier Victorian to country and Western," said Megan. "She didn't stand by her man, so she's a worthless woman. That's not quite right, either, Randal. She did stand by her man while he stood trial for murdering her lover. And was acquitted. But why did he shoot Boyce's father?"

"It was after a Fort Worth court in January of 1912 dismissed charges that Al Boyce, Jr., had abducted Lena from the sanitarium—"

"I should hope so," declared Megan. "It wasn't like it was against Lena's will."

Ryan gave her a searching look as if he doubted her judgment. "Colonel A. G. Boyce, Sr., was sitting in a leather chair in the lobby of the just-completed Metropolitan Hotel when Beal Sneed walked in. The colonel had a reputation for frank speech, and the story goes that he had been holding court in Fort Worth, making such remarks as, if Beal Sneed couldn't control his wife, he deserved to lose her, and calling him spineless. Sneed walked up to A. G., shot six times with a thirty-eight caliber revolver, and only missed him once, and he alleged during his trial that Colonel A. G. Boyce, Sr., assisted in the breakup of his marriage. My grandfather knew A. G. well, and he never believed that allegation. Whatever went on, whatever the machinations were, Al Boyce, Lena, and Sneed kept it between the three of them. I don't believe Al Boyce and Lena needed any assistance, but the people attending the trial for A. G.'s murder definitely took sides. Four men were killed outside the courthouse in disputes over the trial, and women fought one another with hat pins in the halls and even in the courtroom itself. Newspapers from all over the United States and Canada covered the trial—"

"Four men killed and women fighting with hat pins! What an article this will make for one of my professional journals," said Megan. "I might even be able to sell it to one of the popular history magazines that actually pay real money for articles. That is, if anyone believes the story. I'm not sure I believe it. Hat pins! Are you certain of that, Ryan?"

Ryan nodded, a grim expression on his face. "I researched it because it involved ranching history as well as Amarillo history. The *Fort Worth Star-Telegram* reported the fights inside the courthouse and the duels outside the courthouse. The trial, by the way, ended in a mistrial with the jury deadlocked at seven to five for acquittal, but that didn't end the feud. In March of 1912, Beal Sneed's father, Joe T. Sneed, was murdered by a tenant farmer whom the Sneeds believed had been put up to it by the Boyce family. According to my research that wasn't true—the shooting was unrelated to the feud—but Beal Sneed was beyond logical thinking by that time."

"My God! This is an unbelievable story! How did I miss knowing about it? I was born and raised in Amarillo," said Megan.

"By the time you were born, the Boyce family had all left town, and the Sneeds weren't talking about the feud," said Agnes. "And very little has been written about it. Besides, all the murders were over and done with more than sixty years before you were born, and it isn't the sort of material taught in your local history class. It's just us oldsters who were touched by it who remember. And history professors like Ryan."

Megan laid her notebook and pencil down and stood up. "And that's the very reason why I nominate Ryan Stevens to be our guide on our tour of real-life murder sites."

Even over the applause from the members Megan could hear Ryan yelping, "What! Who? Me?"

2

"She looked like a very special kind of dynamite, neatly wrapped in nylon and silk. Only I wasn't having any. I'd been too close to an explosion already. I was powder-shy."

ROBERT YOUNG
(accused murderer Larry Ballantine) about Susan
Hayward (his mistress Verna Carlson),
They Won't Believe Me, 1947

.

My name is Ryan Stevens. I am curator of history at the Panhandle Plains Museum, located on the south side of the campus of West Texas A&M University in Canyon, Texas, where I also teach two courses in American history. The campus is about thirteen-plus miles from Time and Again Bookstore, where I seem to get into one predicament after another. If it's not helping Megan Clark set a trap for a murderer, then it's helping her plan a string figure convention, the highlight of which is murder. This time she wants me to research crime sites in Amarillo—with her help, of course. This can only lead to another predicament. Why do I say that? Because it's inevitable. Put murder, even murder past due, and Megan Clark together, and eventually chaos erupts. I speak from experience. Then why am I involved with Megan Clark, and who exactly is she?

I'll answer the last question first. Megan Clark is actually Dr. Megan Elizabeth Clark, Ph.D. in physical anthropology with a specialty in paleopathology, but until she finds a job doing autopsies on mummies, she is an assistant reference librarian at the downtown branch of the Amarillo Public Library. She is twenty-six years old and cute—although God forbid that anyone would say so—with naturally curly red hair and a sprinkling of freckles across her nose. She is a brilliant scholar, but youth and the Cute Factor, as she calls it, work against her, that and the fact that there aren't many mummies in need of an autopsy. And if a mummy should turn up somewhere, Megan tells me there are forty-nine paleopathologists in line ahead of her. As her mother once told me, Megan never took a single course in college that would enable her to actually make a living, but she does the best she can until her opportunity comes knocking. Her best hope is for a mummy to be found in the Panhandle, so she could be first on site with her diploma, backed up with a copy of her transcript, and her friendship with the Texas state archaeologist. Then she might have a chance.

In the meantime, she works at the library and lives with her mother in a 1920s frame house with a porch on three sides that happens to be next door to me. She's lived there all her life except the eight years she was away at school. For those who wonder, she doesn't live with her mother because she can't cut the apron strings but because it's cheap and she can save her money, so someday she can sponsor her own dig in the Valley of the Kings and duplicate Howard Carter's feat of finding an untouched tomb. Also, not being the domestic type, her mother doesn't have apron strings, symbolic or otherwise. In fact, I'd bet my pension that Megan's mother has never owned an apron in her life, and furthermore, wouldn't recognize one if it turned up on her kitchen table. My wife always used to feed Megan whenever she fed our four children, because she worried that Megan wasn't getting enough to eat, or if her mother did happen to remember to fix a meal, it wasn't nutritious. I never believed that myself. If there is one adjective that describes Megan's mother, it is conscientious. I'm sure she read books on nutrition and provided adequate meals for her daughter according to planned menus. What she didn't provide was a cozy family atmosphere, but that wasn't her fault. I always thought motherhood was something that crept up on her when she had her mind on other issues, and she never quite developed the knack for it. It didn't help that Megan's dad died when she was five. I always thought she was closer to him. But to sum up, Megan grew up mostly at my house, she was my oldest daughter's best friend, and after I was widowed and she moved back to Amarillo, she became mine. She's still my best friend, but sometime over the summer, I realized I love her as well.

I've never told her and probably never will.

Why am I involved with her? How did it start? I'm nineteen years older than she, so one would assume I'm a father figure. I'm not. Any father figure of Megan's would need to be proficient with tools and auto mechanics, with camping—she can start a fire by rubbing two sticks together—with rock climbing, with all other manner of outdoor activities. I can't say that I qualify. The internal combustion engine is a mystery to me, I'm allergic to sage and mesquite—and there's no place in the Panhandle of Texas without sage and mesquite—so camping gives me terrible sinus attacks, and the last time I went rock climbing with her, I fell and broke my wrist. So why does she put up with me? Because I am her best friend, just as she is mine. Sometimes friendships don't make sense when viewed from the outside.

So my involvement with Megan began with friendship and a shared history dating back to her childhood. It is only in the last six months that our relationship has taken an interesting turn. I have become Megan's Watson. From my observations and what might best be called Megan's field notes—brief, very often pithy jottings about people, places, and things—I write up our adventures in crime fighting. One day I hope to have my scribbling published, as I've always had a secret desire to write, although I never thought I would be writing true crime. My ambitions were to be the next Louis L'Amour as I was, am, and always will be a rabid fan of Westerns. Not that I can brag about it, not with the current flock of revisionist historians waiting to pounce upon *anyone* who admits to reading Westerns, much less a full professor of American history. To hear the shrill cackles from the revisionist camp, one would think that Max Brand, Ernest Haycox, Louis L'Amour, and A. B. Guthrie, Jr., wrote child pornography, and Elmer Kelton and Richard S. Wheeler are carrying on the tradition.

But let me return to the subject of Megan Clark and her faithful Watson. To those who wonder why the elder statesman of the duo takes the position of recording secretary rather than leader, Megan possesses certain skills necessary for a Sherlock Holmes, and I don't. Megan can look at a body dead by unnatural causes and analyze the crime scene, picking out all the anomalies. Like most anthropologists/archaeologists, Megan can reconstruct a scene using a minimum of clues. I look at a dead body, particularly if it is in a "seeping" stage, and I faint. I have gained quite a reputation among the law enforcement community for my ability to sustain a deep faint until dragged away from the vicinity of the body. As for reconstructing a crime scene, one must remain conscious to do that.

All this does not mean I'm a coward, or spineless, or a sissy, or a wimp; it means I'm a Watson, and I'm satisfied with the position.

However, my above discussion should not be construed to mean that I approve of Megan's extracurricular sleuthing any more than my grandfather really approved of Beal Sneed. Murder investigations are best left to the police, and amateur sleuths are best left between the covers of a book. But once circumstances set events in motion, as Lena Sneed's confession set off a feud, then one must choose a side. Once Megan stumbles over a dead body, then I must play my part, controlling such of her illegal activities as I know about ahead of time— breaking and entering comes to mind—and subduing her instincts to solve the puzzle as best I can. My score so far is Ryan Stevens: zero; Megan Clark: two.

What I cannot do is turn my back on Megan and walk away.

"The only murders I know anything about are the Boyce-Sneed killings, and the only reason I know about those is because it's part of ranching history. The study of murder is not my avocation as it is with certain other individuals I could mention—mainly, every member of Murder by the Yard. It chills my blood the way two well-bred old ladies like Rosemary and Lorene can discuss the most bloodcurdling murders without turning a blue-tinted hair."

We were sitting in my study, a room with four walls of bookshelves and the minimum of furniture, mainly one large desk with high-backed office chair, two upholstered easy chairs, and two floor lamps. The furniture sits in the middle of the room so it won't interfere with finding a necessary book. I was behind my desk with my feet crossed and resting on top of its surface. There is a shallow dent in the right-hand corner that just matches the right heel of my Justin boot. Megan, as usual, was pacing, carefully stepping over such stacks of books as were present. I had just finished my research and lecture notes for my evening seminar on George Armstrong Custer and the Battle of the Little Big Horn, so there were more books than usual scattered about. I work more on the pile system than the file system until a project is done. Then I put everything neatly away until I began a new pile for a new project. I hadn't gotten to the putting-away stage of my Custer project, so the stacks were numerous and high. You would not believe how much is written about Custer in a single year, much less the cumulative number of pages written in the hundred-plus years since June 1876. There has been enough ink spilled on Custer to fill a medium-size pond. Megan tells me that makes Custer a rival of Sherlock Holmes. Despite her assurances, I find it hard to believe that there are nearly as many scholarly papers on a man who didn't exist as there are on the worst defeat in the history of the frontier army.

But to get back to my subject. Megan was pacing my study, waving her hands about as she spoke, which she always does when we're alone. Otherwise, she tries to control her physical exuberance, since she says hand gestures while speaking is not quite acceptable in American culture.

"The Twins do not have blue-tinted hair, Ryan."

"I was exaggerating to make a point."

She gave me a sharp look. In any country except

America, an anthropologist/archaeologist is a scientist. Here, the two disciplines are lumped together in the liberal arts or social sciences departments of almost all American colleges and universities. Megan considers social sciences to be an oxymoron. At any rate, she believes exaggeration unacceptable in a serious discussion. I just couldn't believe what we were having was a serious discussion.

"What I'm trying to say is that I'm unsuited to whatever tour you have in mind. I don't even read mysteries, for God's sake! Get Randal to do it."

"Randal would irritate the audience."

"Then ask Call Me Herb."

"Herb would put the audience to sleep."

"Not necessarily. Not if he didn't read those chapters from his work in progress."

"Trust me on this, Ryan. You're the only one who can do this. You're a professor—"

"So are you!"

"No one would take me seriously. The Cute Factor, you know. But as I was saying you're a professor, you have silver in your sideburns—"

"Thanks a lot!"

". . . So you're mature, you're photogenic—those killer blue eyes will look gorgeous on a poster advertising the event—and you're well known as a local historian. I think we'll do the publicity shot for the poster in film noir style. You can wear a trench coat and fedora, like Humphrey Bogart. Lorene can dress like a parson's wife with a modest coat and hat, and Rosemary can be the society matron with multiple strings of pearls and a lorgnette. Candi will be the maid holding the tea tray; Randal can wear a loud tweed suit as the police inspector—there is always a police inspector—and Herb can be the reporter with a card that says Press tucked in his hatband and one of those old-fashioned cameras with the flash attachment."

"And just what role are you going to play, missy?" I asked.

"I'll be the slinky femme fatale in the low-cut satin and beaded dress with the feather in her hair. I do slinky well. It's my coloring, I think. It looks dramatic on film."

The thought of Megan dressed in a low-cut, sleek, tight satin gown with beads to refract the light from all the curves of her body made me break out in a sweat.

"Over my dead body," I said without thinking. A mistake.

She gave me an odd look, in between suspicious and surprised, like she wasn't sure what I was talking about. She had been giving me frequent looks of those kind lately. "You don't want to be in the picture? But, Ryan, we need you. You're the one who will lecture at each site. You'll provide the background information the audience needs before they watch my dramatic scenario. Besides, no one else has such killer blue eyes."

"Don't think you can soften me up with compliments, Megan. And why do we need posters, anyway? You said you would pass out press releases. That means a sheet of paper with no pictures, so *if* the media mentions us, they will have the facts, and *if* anybody is interested in going on the tour, they can join Murder by the Yard. I don't recall any mention of posters or dramatic scenarios. Exactly what kind of dramatic scenario did you have in mind?"

I saw her swallow, and her eyes skittered over my shoulder toward the bookcase that held my Louis L'Amour collection. Any time Megan doesn't meet your eyes, she has some plan that is, to use an expression she picked up when she spent her junior year in college in Scotland, dodgy. A loose equivalent would be our expression: something up her sleeve.

"You already know so much about the Boyce-Sneed feud, and I'll help you do research on the other crimes. You provide me with the correct locations and the facts, and I'll write a dramatic scenario of the murder. We can stage it like those murder weekends I'm always reading about. Just think of the new members we might have join, and . . . and think of Agnes. She really needs a broader customer base, Ryan. There are lots of other used bookstores in Amarillo she has to compete with, and she's never done anything except run Time and Again. If her business goes bankrupt, what would she do? How would she live?" She finally looked me in the eye, her expression guileless. Nobody does guileless like Megan.

"For one thing, she could sell her property on Sixth Street for about a quarter of a million dollars, sock it away in mutual funds, and live off the earnings with plenty for beans and bacon and occasional beer. Ever since Route 66 nostalgia has become a national pastime, any property on Sixth Street, which I might remind you is the original Route 66 through Amarillo, has been worth a fortune. So Agnes might not want to sell her bookstore, and I personally don't want her to, but she wouldn't starve to death."

"You don't need to remind me about Sixth Street and Route 66," said Megan, a frown putting wrinkles in her forehead. "But you're missing the point."

"The point being?" I asked, clasping my hands behind my head and leaning back in my chair. It's not often that I get the best of Megan, and I intended to enjoy it while I could.

She looked at me out of those light brown eyes of hers—whiskey-colored eyes, if one wants a poetic turn of phrase—and clasped her hands under her chin. She was wearing a black tank top, a long, filmy, black wraparound skirt with tiny white flowers on it—daisies, I think—and a pair of thick soled sandals with clunky heels—a change from her usual cutoffs, Texas crew T-shirt, and hiking boots. With the subject being murder, and her pose, like an innocent supplicant, it wouldn't take much imagination on my part to feel like Humphrey Bogart meeting a Generation X Lauren Bacall. I almost opened my bottom desk drawer to see if it held a half-empty bottle of whiskey. And come to think of it, Bogart had been twenty or so years older than Bacall.

I broke out in a sweat again, lifted my feet off the desk, and stood up. I cleared my throat and gave thanks that she couldn't hear my rapid heartbeat. "It's getting late, Megan, and we both have to work tomorrow, so whatever argument you were going to use can wait."

"It's not that late, and you never go to bed before midnight, anyway."

"How do you know that?"

"I can see your bedroom window from my room. It never goes dark before midnight. You're making excuses because you don't want to be involved with Murder by the Yard. I've known it from the beginning, I just didn't want to admit it to myself. But it's all right, Ryan. It was nice of you to come with me as long as you did, but you don't have to anymore. I understand."

Somewhere in that speech I was being flummoxed—I knew it—but I couldn't stop my response. "I never said I didn't enjoy coming with you to Murder by the Yard, and I have no intention of dropping out, and not because I'm being nice. That makes me sound like some sweet old uncle taking you to the zoo. I just don't want to be your tour guide. Aren't I entitled to say no?"

Megan gave me a little half smile over her shoulder—like Lauren Bacall in *The Big Sleep*—as she paused in the doorway. "Of course. We're friends. Friends can tell each other no, can't they?"

I couldn't see any trap in that question, so I answered. "That's why friends are friends. I'm sure Herb or Randal will do fine as tour guide."

She shook her head. "No, I've thought about it, and I don't think so. Herb would want to wear a vest, and Randal still confuses sarcasm with humor. I think I'll ask Jerry Carr instead. He would do it just so I would forgive him for suspecting me of murder."

Adrenaline rushed through my body. "Jerry?" I asked, my voice a low growl I didn't recognize. "That would be Lieutenant Jerry Carr of Special Crimes?"

"I don't know any other Jerry Carr, do you?"

I didn't, but I wished like hell I did. The particular Jerry Carr we both knew was in his early thirties—very early thirties—much closer to Megan's age than I, and good looking in a square-jawed, hawk-nosed, Dick Tracy sort of way. He and Megan had dated until he suspected her of murder last spring. Megan took umbrage at his suspicions, and I rejoiced. I know I'm unsuitable to be Megan's lover, but that doesn't mean I'm not jealous. I am. Green with it. I know it's unworthy of me, but I'm not unselfish enough to wish her well in someone else's arms. I should love her more, so I would be happy if she found a man her own age she loved. Or I should love her less, so it wouldn't hurt so much when she did. I can't seem to do either.

"He doesn't have killer blue eyes," I said.

"No, he doesn't," she agreed.

"He wouldn't look as good in a fedora."

"I don't think so, either."

"All right, I'll be your tour guide."

She danced around my desk and hugged me. "Thank you, Ryan! You're my best friend in the world."

I put my hands on her shoulders and pushed her away so I could see her face. Until that moment, I didn't realize how much bare flesh a tank top revealed. I felt my heartbeat pick up. "You manipulated me."

She smiled that Lauren Bacall smile again. "You would have been sorry if I had gone ahead without you. What if I got into trouble? You wouldn't be around to rescue me."

"I don't recall ever rescuing you before. You seem to do a good enough job of rescuing yourself." I turned her around and pushed her gently toward the door. "Go home before you get into trouble."

She looked around. "I'm in your office. What kind of trouble could I get into—unless I knocked over one of your stacks of books."

I gave her my best Humphrey Bogart stare. "When you're in Philip Marlowe's office, you never know what might happen."

She laughed and waltzed out of my office. I followed her to the door and watched her cross the lawn to her own house. I leaned against the door frame and wiped my sweaty face on my sleeve. My adrenaline rush was over, and in its place chills walked up my spine on icy feet. I saw a predicament yawning before me.

MURDER IN SELF-DEFENSE: THE CASE OF SHERIFF GOBER

"The first man indicted for murder in Potter County was its first sheriff, a fresh-faced young man named James Gober, who ran afoul of the county commissioners' court and its uncrowned king, Jim Holland. According to Gober's memoirs, Holland pledged the county to pay forty-eight thousand dollars to build a new courthouse, when in fact experts tell Gober that materials and labor would amount to only twelve thousand dollars at most. Gober immediately passes along this information to certain of Amarillo's taxpayers. Holland and his cronies on the commissioners' court retaliate by hiring a man named M. M. Givens as constable, a killer and hired gun according to Clabe Merchant, Gober's only friend on the court, who warns the young sheriff to watch his back. Barely does the commisioners' court adjourn than Givens confronts young Gober. Anticipating Givens' actions when he sees the gunfighter put his hand on his gun, a big, shiny .44, Gober draws his own .45 Colt and tells Given that he'll have to do his job another time or tell Holland to take care of his own dirty work. That was the situation the afternoon of January 10, 1889.

Imagine the young sheriff sitting alone on the hotel porch after his first confrontation with M. M. Givens, knowing he has no proof that elected public officials have hired a gunslinger to kill him. His only ally on the commissioners' court, Clabe Merchant, by no means a powerless individual in the community, is afraid of Holland and his crooked bunch. "Watch your back," he tells the young man, but cautions Gober not to repeat what he says, and the sheriff gives his word. Merchant's warning saves Gober's life in the first confrontation, but what about the next, and the one after that? Who would help him?

He sits on the hotel porch of the Amarillo House in the cool January afternoon, not moving, not speaking to anyone, sick at heart and dreading another meeting with Givens. He was sheriff of Potter County and had always been square with every man he met. He will not back down from Givens and the crooked dealings of the commissioners' court, but God help him, because someone will die—either him or Givens."

His friend, John Hollicott, the manager of the LX ranch, drove up to the hotel and asked him to come have a drink. Gober, feeling low as he has ever felt in his life, his eyes wet from tears shed at his situation, at first refuses because he pledged not to drink at the bar for six months. Hollicott asks him to have a beer instead in the back room of L. B. Collins's saloon which adjoins the hotel. Gober accepts, and gets up from his chair on the hotel porch. He is tense, and stiff from having sat so long, and attempts to walk off his stiffness in the short ten steps to Collins's saloon. When they enter the back room, the gambling room, Givens is there threatening to run the twelve or so gamblers out of town if they didn't pay him seventeen dollars each. Gober stops by the door and puts his right hand on the short .45 Colt he always carries in the left side of his waistband under his coat.

Givens wheels around and goes for his gun while Gober points with his left hand, shouting for Givens not to draw. There is only a split second to stop the inevitable, and Gober knows it, knows also the die is cast. Givens draws, but he is slower than Gober whose bullet cuts through the gunslinger's spine. Givens falls, still clutching the .44. Gober disarms him and helps the mortally wounded Givens next door to the Tremont Hotel.

That is how Gober relates the incident in his memoirs. Other accounts vary. Givens, for example, was elected constable in November of 1888, not appointed in January of 1889, but obviously there was bad blood between Givens and Gober. Despite the best efforts of Holland and his cronies on the commissioners' court, Jim Gober was found not guilty at his trial for murder, but was denied his victory in the next election, as the commissioners court refused his bond, declared the office of sheriff vacant, and appointed another man."

Drs. Ryan Stevens and Megan Clark on the case of James Gober, the first person indicted for murder in Amarillo, Texas, January 14, 1889.

3

"When I get excited about something, I give it everything I've got. I'm funny that way."

LAUREN BACALL
(artist Irene Jansen) to Humphrey Bogart (escaped
con Vincent Parry),
Dark Passage, 1947

Megan sat in the front passenger seat of Herb's motor home, checked her notes on her clipboard, and cleared her throat. "I think we're ready, but let's go over the schedule one more time. "We leave at precisely ten. Ryan will be driving, since he is the narrator and won't be taking a role in any of the scenarios. The living room of the motor home is the men's dressing room, and the bedroom is the ladies'. Does everyone have their costumes ready?"

"We all have our costumes, Megan. We have the few props we'll use to set the scene. We know our lines, both the historical ones we can validate and the ones you've added in the name of dramatic license. We know who we're playing and what to do, so would you dispense with going over your notes again? I, for one, have them memorized." Randal, dressed in an old-fashioned black suit with string tie, Stetson, and a facsimile Potter County sheriff's badge pinned on his coat, looked around at the other members of Murder by the Yard gathered behind the motor home's front seats. "Does anybody need to hear another run-through from our director?"

"We'll be going to Parker and Third Street first for the Jim Gober scenario. Is that correct, Megan?" asked Herb Jackson, looking over Lorene's shoulder. Herb was also dressed in an old-fashioned suit, this one brown, with a stained and embroidered waistcoat, a .45 revolver strapped around his waist, and an unshaven chin.

Megan was willing to bid her first mummy that Herbert Jackson III had never failed in this life to shave until this morning, but as M. M. Givens, Herb thought he needed to look a little more like a thug and a little less like a lawyer. Not that they knew for sure Givens was a thug, but a dramatic scenario needs a focus, and in this scenario its focus was Jim Gober, hero. "That's right, Herb. Now remember, everybody, this scenario requires the round, drop-leaf table and the wooden chairs to suggest the gambling room. We'll set those up in front of the storage building near the end of the block on the west side of Parker, since that's where the saloon originally was. I wish we had flats with appropriate backgrounds painted on them, but with so few people to carry flats to and from the motor home and so little space, it just wasn't practical."

"I'm surprised you let practicalities get in the way of this three-ring circus," muttered Ryan under his breath.

Megan heard him and glared. He had been acting like a bear with a sore paw ever since the first television van showed up. "We'll have to rely on the audience's imagination instead. Now, where was I? Oh, yes, the Tremont Hotel was next door to the south, where the metal building is now, and we'll need three folding chairs to suggest the veranda. We'll take volunteers from the tour bus for the gamblers, but Candi, you're the saloon girl and Rosemary is the madam, and Candi, don't forget the cards and play money." Both ladies waved their hands in acknowledgment. "Lorene, you and Agnes are the respectable matrons sitting on the veranda of the hotel where you've been watching young Jim Gober as he reflects upon the commissioners' court hiring a gunslinger to kill him, and a few squeals when you hear the shot won't be out of place. Ryan and I aren't in this scenario, so we'll help set up the props and select volunteers for the gamblers."

"Ryan is not in this scenario, and furthermore, if I had known you were turning this into a Hollywood production, Ryan wouldn't be anywhere near Third and Parker, or any of the other sites," Ryan leaned over from his position in the driver's seat to whisper in Megan's ear. "Remind me to get a strict definition of your terminology before I sign on another one of your little gigs. Dramatic scenario, my left buttock! This is a three-act play, with props and extras! And have you noticed the press? They're crawling all over the place like—like bees in search of honey. I tried to go back in the bookstore to go to the bathroom—since Rosemary and Candi were occupying the one in the motor home—and some blonde reporter from Channel 10 stuck a microphone in my face."

He leaned back in the driver's seat of the motor home and glared at Megan. She looked out the window at the vans and SUVs crowding the parking lot of Time and Again Bookstore, each with a logo of either a TV channel, a radio station, or in the case of one car, the *Amarillo Globe News*, and debated whether she should act surprised or not. Probably not, since Ryan wouldn't believe her, so she might as well tell the truth.

"Of course, I've noticed the press! Didn't you see me talking to the reporters?"

"I saw you handing out those posters—as if they weren't already plastered all over town. I caught a student of mine with one pinned on his backpack."

Megan ignored him, which sometimes was the best way to handle Ryan when he was in one of his moods. "And isn't it wonderful that all four TV stations are represented? And three radio stations, and the newspaper! We have my mother to thank for that."

"I could have figured that," said Ryan, glowering at her.

"She knows how to get press coverage from all those years fighting the DOE over the high-level nuclear waste dump the bureaucrats wanted to locate in Deaf Smith County. And other causes, of course. Anyway, she gave me some hints. I have interviews with different cast members—er, reading circle members—set up for each representative of the media. My mother recommended that. She said that way all the TV and radio stations and the newspaper would have a different story, they wouldn't compete with one another, and the coverage of the event would be excellent. I have you scheduled for a newspaper interview at the last stop on Polk Street where we do the Boyce-Sneed bit."

"I am not speaking to the newspaper, television, or radio!"

"Why not?"

Ryan's mouth worked for several seconds before he found his voice. "Because I was misled!"

"I told you I wanted to do the scenarios like a mystery weekend," retorted Megan. "What did you think I meant? That you and I would stand around doing dramatic readings?"

"What would I know about a mystery weekend?" he shouted, then caught himself and lowered his voice to a whisper. "I read Westerns, not mysteries."

"Which you obviously don't want the rest of the reading circle to know. Are you ashamed of your literary taste?"

"Are you blackmailing me?" he asked with a look that for some reason reminded Megan of Humphrey Bogart in *The Maltese Falcon.*

"All right, Ryan! If you're going to be stubborn, forget it. I just thought since you were the narrator and did so much research on these old murders that you would be the perfect person to give the interview, but I'll ask Randal instead."

"You're not manipulating me again, Angel."

"What did you call me?" asked Megan, feeling bewildered—and Ryan never bewildered her—except maybe the few times he called her honey.

"I called you Angel because you've got that half smile on your face like Lauren Bacall in *The Big Sleep.*"

"Ryan! I didn't know you ever watched any of those old film noirs."

Ryan poked his chest with his thumb. "You don't know everything about me, Angel."

"That sounds more like a Bacall line," said Megan.

Randal poked his head between the two. "If you two don't stop arguing, you're not going to have anything left to argue about. In case you hadn't noticed—and I bet you haven't—the natives are getting restless. We've already had two old ladies get off the tour bus, and Agnes has had to refund their money."

"Watch it with the remarks about old ladies, Randal," said Rosemary, poking him in the ribs.

"Just drive, Ryan. We can argue later," said Megan,

sitting down in the passenger seat and picking up the microphone to the PA system she had rigged up from various bits and pieces of audio equipment left over from her mother's last cause. "Ladies and gentlemen, if you will follow us, our first stop will be at Third and Parker, the original town site of Amarillo, where we will reenact the shooting of Constable M. M. Givens by Sheriff James Gober, January tenth, 1889."

Megan stood with her back to the original Potter County courthouse at Fifth and Bowie, a few blocks from the site of the hotel where Constable M. M. Givens died a few days after being shot at the saloon next door. The courthouse had changed over time from its original look. It no longer had a third story and a cupola but it still had a fence and the original brick and mortar gate, fences and gates being necessary to keep stray cattle and hogs away from the seat of government. It was a brick building, rather large, which had been stuccoed over and painted a color between brown and salmon. The building had a feeling of history about it, as though the aging courthouse still dreamed of earlier days when the sounds of horses' hooves and buggy wheels echoed in the dusty streets of old Amarillo, and the sulfur smell of gunpowder all too often gave the evening air an unneeded scent.

Megan cleared her throat and straightened her shoulders. Several cameras flashed as participants on the tour took her picture.

"In the building behind me, a grand jury met and returned an indictment against James Gober. It read as follows: 'In the Name and by the Authority of the State of Texas: The Grand Jurors, good and lawful men of the State of Texas, County of Potter, duly tried on oath by the Judge of the District Court of said County touching

their legal qualifications as Grand Jurors, elected, im-
paneled, sworn and charged at the March Term, 1889,
of the District Court of Potter County, Texas, to inquire
into and true presentment make of all offenses against
the penal laws of said State, committed within the body
of the County aforesaid, upon their oaths present to the
District Court of said County, that James R. Gober, Late
of the County of Potter, on the 10th day of January in
the year of our Lord one thousand eight hundred and
eighty nine, with force and arms, in the County of Potter
and State of Texas, did then and there with malice afore-
thought, kill and murder one M. M. Givens by there and
then shooting him, the aforesaid M. M. Givens, with a
pistol.' "

Megan folded the photocopy of the original indictment and put it at the bottom of the stack of similar
photocopies on her clipboard. She cleared her throat
again and smiled at the crowd of people making the tour.
"Are there any questions before we drive on to Amarillo
Boulevard and the site of the Tex Thornton murder?"

An elderly gentleman with a full head of silver hair
and the aged remains of what had once been spectacular
good looks, raised his right hand while he held tightly
to a cane with his other. Megan recognized him as the
volunteer who had played the part of LX manager John
Hollicott in their dramatic scenario.

"Excuse me, Dr. Clark, but what do you really believe? Did Gober walk into that back room with the intention of killing Givens? Can we really trust his
acquittal, since his father-in-law was the district judge,
even though he excused himself from presiding over
Gober's trial? And you did say Givens had been elected
in November, not appointed the morning of January
tenth as Gober says. Give us an analysis."

Megan swallowed. She had not anticipated such questions on this—one of the least ambiguous cases—particularly when she had written her scenario to support the cause of Jim Gober. Where was this old man coming from, anyway? It was her generation, Generation X, with the reputation for cynicism, not his.

"Of course, we have Gober's memoir, and it is always to one's advantage to outlive your opponents and leave a written record of your side of events, but allowing for the fact that Jim Gober was an elderly man when he recorded his memories, I would say that errors are due to forgetfulness rather than the deliberate intention to mislead. Killing a man leaves an indelible impression upon the mind, and I believe Gober recorded events as he best remembered their happening. I believe there was a meeting of the commissioners' court on January tenth, and that Givens attended. Maybe Clabe Merchant warned Gober that day that Givens was going to kill him at the first opportunity with the unspoken blessings of the commissioners' court, or maybe he had warned him sometime earlier. At any rate, Gober knew his life was at risk. I further believe that there was a confrontation between Givens and Jim Gober immediately after that meeting, and that confrontation was the motive for Jim Gober to sit on the hotel veranda for two hours.

"He was waiting for that meeting, that next confrontation that would turn deadly, when John Hollicott invited him for a drink. He didn't want to leave the veranda and gave a rather lame excuse that he had taken a pledge not to drink over the bar for six months. Of Gober's account of that afternoon, that is his only statement that I don't wholly believe. I think he knew that Givens was in the bar. How could he help but know? The hotel was only ten steps from the saloon. He had to have seen Givens go into that saloon. He didn't want to confront Givens in a crowded saloon where other people might be hurt and where he didn't have the advantage. Saloons were crowded and dark and smoky even during the day, not a good place for a gunfight. Remember, Gober agreed to have a beer in the *back* room, or gambling room of the saloon. I don't think he expected Givens to be there, and when he was, Gober stayed by the door with his back against the wall. I also believe Gober's account of Givens' hassling the gamblers for "seventeen dollars each," or he would run them out of town. That is such an odd amount that it is believable. Givens's supporters later said he was passing out warrants for gambling, and according to the evidence, he was. Give me a break! There was gambling in every saloon in Old Town. Why pick on this particular saloon? Because Gober frequented it. I believe the warrants were a ploy to get Gober in L. B. Collins' saloon. Another indication that the business of the warrants is specious is the fact that Givens refused to say who signed them. What is clear from all the witnesses is that Givens, angry because the gamblers and bystanders were arguing with him, drew his gun and pointed it at Gober, who *nobody* testified as having taken part in the argument. As much as Gober's times and some of his locations are off, his essential story is, I believe, true."

The silver-haired elderly gentleman bowed slightly and smiled. "A wonderful analysis, Dr. Clark, and I suspect it is as accurate as can be, given the fact that it all actual happened in the century before last. And we must remember we're now in the twenty-first century, a long time from our pioneer beginnings. Or are we? Do you think the passions and lust and greed of the nineteenth century are any different from ours?"

She felt Ryan whisper in her ear. "Better wrap it up, Angel. We're way behind schedule, and if we don't hurry, we'll be doing the Boyce-Sneed case under the streetlights."

She patted his arm and hoped he wouldn't bite her hand off, given his mood. "Let me answer this question, and we'll be on our way."

She smiled at the elderly man, who reminded her of someone, she just couldn't remember who. "I'm an anthropologist and an archaeologist, and I can guarantee you that human behavior has remained consistent over the millennia. Perhaps you should come to one of our meetings of Murder by the Yard at the Time and Again Bookstore on Sixth Street, and we'll continue our discussion. But for now, the Tex Thornton case beckons. Remember, everyone, there's no dramatic scenario for this one. Not only is it an R-rated murder, it's too brutal to act out in broad daylight on Amarillo Boulevard East."

THE END OF A LEGEND: THE MURDER OF TEX THORNTON

On a sleepy Wednesday afternoon of June 22, 1949, a Texas legend walked into the San Jon Bar, located in the town of the same name in New Mexico. W. A. "Tex" Thornton made his living fighting oil well fires, but what made him a legend was when he allegedly broke a four-year drought in Dalhart, Texas, in 1935, by tying dynamite onto balloons and exploding them in the clouds. Torrance Popejoy, the bar's proprietor, was an old friend of Tex's and watched the subsequent actions of Tex and the young couple accompanying him more closely than a stranger might. Popejoy particularly noticed the young woman: a tall, slender, beautiful blonde woman who looked to be in her early twenties. Her companion was shorter and wore a white baseball hat. Tex ordered two rounds of whisky sours, although the young man drank only beer, then the three climbed into the front seat of Tex's 1948 black Chrysler sedan. The last time Popejoy saw his friend, Tex was sitting by the passenger side door and the young man was driving east toward Amarillo. Around 8:00 that evening the three stopped for gas at Briggs Service Station in Adrian, 50 miles west of Amarillo. Tex Thornton appeared intoxicated to the service station attendant. It was nearly dark, around 8:30, when the three pulled into the Park Plaza Motel at 612 N.E. Eighth Avenue which is the present-day Amarillo Boulevard East.

Imagine a gray stuccoed building, with the office a two-storied hump on one end with the entrance to the interior courtyard beside it. To the left of the office the building is one story, with colorful striped awnings over the windows and a landscaped grassy strip in front. It is not a particularly fancy motel, but it is brand new, clean and well-kept, and does boast of having refrigerated air. It is the sort of place a well-know local might take a hitch-hiking couple to impress them without running the risk of being recognized, particularly since the motel boasted an interior courtyard where passing traffic could not see Tex Thornton's black Chrysler. The young woman registered, signing her name as E. O. Johnson of Detroit, Michigan, and paying $8.50 for a two-bedroom cabin. Tex Thornton undoubtedly paid for the room although he didn't sign the register, nor did he get out of the car where he might be seen by local residents eating at the popular Rice's Dining Salon across the street. The motel building is gone now, replaced by two other businesses, and few probably remember the Plaza Park Motel or what happened there.

At 10:00, the young couple climbed into the black Chrysler, asked the motel porter, Charlie Thompson, for a push to get the car started and drove east on Route 66 toward Oklahoma. At approximately 9:15 the next morning, Jessie Mae Walker, a motel maid, found Thornton's nude body in the back bedroom of the cabin. His shirt was bound tightly around his neck and savage blows to the head had shattered his skull. Blood had soaked through the mattress and pooled under the bed. Thornton's wallet and identification were gone, along with whatever money he was carrying, and he was reputed to always carry a lot of cash. Other than Thornton's body and blood, clues in the room included a bloody pair of trousers with the name R. L. Leach written inside the waistband, empty beer cans, dirty glasses, a handkerchief with lipstick smeared on it, and evidence of blood in the bathroom sink where the killer had washed himself. The Chrysler was traced to Dodge City, and the trousers to the Salvation Army in Colorado Springs. For eight months it was a perfect crime as every lead led nowhere-until February 7, 1950, when a young blonde woman named Diana Heaney Johnson turned herself into the police in Washington, D.C., and told Amarillo authorities where to find her husband, Evald Johnson, whom she accused of beating Tex Thornton to death.

What happened inside that two-bedroom cabin? Did Evald Johnson act as a pimp for his wife, then change his mind and beat Thornton to death? Or did Evald Johnson commit a justifiable homicide in defense of his marriage as he claimed at his trial? Or did young Diana, seventeen at the time of the murder and on her own since she ran away from home at fifteen, seduce the local legend after her husband passed out from heavy drinking, in hopes of getting some of the cash Tex carried, and just had the bad luck to be caught by her husband? And what of his story that Diana stole Thornton's money and Johnson knew nothing about it until later? Diana's stories change with the reporter. First Evald beat Tex with his own .45, then she said she beat him with a hammer. Where did he get the hammer? There was no hammer found at the scene. What really happened that hot June night? Did Diana go out to the car and return to find her husband beating Tex to death? Or did Evald Johnson wake up to see his nude wife walking toward the back of the cabin? Johnson claimed he followed his wife, caught her in bed with Thornton, took Thornton's gun away from him, and used it as a blunt instrument. Did Thornton have seduction in mind when he drove within two hundred feet of his own home to check into a motel with strangers? Or was he looking for a place to "sleep it off" because his wife nagged him about his drinking as she testified at Johnson's trial?

And what of the lipstick-smeared handkerchief found at the murder scene? In those days almost all women blotted their lipstick. Did Diana apply lipstick and drop her hanky next to Thornton's dead body, or did she kiss someone and wipe lipstick off his face? Whose face? Her husband's? Unlikely, since the owner of the San Jon Bar said the two weren't affectionate. So it must have been Thornton's and the handkerchief is evidence of inappropriate behavior on the part of Thornton or Diana. Did he grab her and kiss her? Or did she kiss him? Either way it is unlikely Evald Johnson would have stood by without acting. Some event triggered the violence of that night. And despite Diana's claims that her husband was brutal to her, she made no effort to run to the motel office for help, nor did she indicate fear when she and Evald left. One suspects that the roll of cash that Tex reputedly carried had a lot to do with the couple's seeming calm.

Another question that remains unanswered and perhaps always will is why Diana turned herself in. It was a perfect crime. The authorities had no idea who had committed the murder. Was Diana tired of living on the run, or was she angry with Evald, or did her conscience hurt her? Or was it because the first to "roll over" for a crime generally gets the best deal, and Diana Heaney Johnson got a superb deal? Murder charges were dropped, she received a probated four-year sentence for transporting a stolen vehicle across state lines, a crime for which Johnson served four years, and she basked in media attention. What would Diana say if she were still alive and someone asked her what happened that night of June 22, 1949?

Drs. Ryan Stevens and Megan Clark on the murder of legendary Tex Thornton.

4

"There are eight million stories in the naked city. This had been one of them."

VOICE-OVER NARRATOR
(Mark Hellinger)
The Naked City, 1948

I was numb. No, that's incorrect. I throbbed from the top of my head, which threatened to explode at any second, to the bottoms of my feet, which burned as if they had been set on fire. The right side of my face had first-degree burns from standing too close to the fake bomb in the A. D. Payne scenario. My back ached, my joints creaked, my voice was hoarse, and every time I closed my eyes, flashbulbs went off. My killer blue eyes were rimmed in red, my broad shoulders slumped, and my butt felt as though it would drop off any second. For once I was glad Megan had driven us to Time and Again this morning, which in the face of my physical miseries seemed at least a year ago. I wondered if I could lie down in the bed of her behemoth pickup for the ride home rather than sitting in the passenger seat. Besides the fact that riding with Megan is an adventure under any circumstances, since she can barely see over the steering wheel, her pickup has a bench seat, which is always locked into the position closest to the dashboard. A tall person, which at over six feet I am, has a choice of riding with his knees tucked nearly under his chin, or sideways, in which case the seat belt has a stranglehold on his torso. I wasn't sure I could tolerate either position, given the extent of my miseries. In fact, I wasn't certain I could get up from Agnes's couch in the reading area of Time and Again. But I would have to manage or look old and decrepit in Megan's eyes, and I would rather not do that with Jerry Carr only a phone call away. I once asked Megan if it bothered her to have a much older friend, and she said as an anthropologist slash archaeologist, she loved old things.

I don't think she was answering my question from quite the same perspective in which I had asked it.

The silver-haired man who had asked Megan about James Gober shooting M. M. Givens was sitting in an easy chair next to me, filling out a questionnaire. I didn't remember filling out a questionnaire when I joined Murder by the Yard, but Megan may have filled it out for me. She often takes the lead in these minor matters. She takes the lead in major matters if I don't watch her.

And speaking of Megan, she was tapping her fingers on the arm of the couch. That is always a bad sign because it means her restless mind is thinking up another project.

"I think the tour was a hit with everyone, don't you, Agnes?" Megan asked the proprietor of Time and Again.

"Oh, definitely! I sold so many books, both this morning before we started the tour and afterward, that I can pay the taxes and all the utilities for the rest of this year and half of next. And now that Sixth Street is high-priced real estate, thanks to the Route 66 craze, my taxes are no small amount. Several people asked if they could visit Murder by the Yard to see if they would like a mystery reading club before they joined. And the money we took in from the tour will reimburse Rosemary and Lorene for the refreshments they provide every week. In fact, we may have enough in the kitty to all go to dinner one night. I wish we could have a tour every year, but I suppose we would run out of murder sites."

"Certainly we would run out of interesting murders," said Megan. "And we would have to start including more recent murders, which would upset the victims' families, and I don't want to do that. I have a suggestion, though."

I knew it! Megan's finger tapping always precluded trouble. I turned cold at the thought of another of her suggestions. I had just barely survived the result of her last brainchild. If I had stood any closer to that fake bomb, I'd be looking at the possibilities of skin grafts.

"I think we should choose one unsolved crime each year after the tour to study. We could devote one meeting of our four each month to discuss our progress toward the solution. We could read the newspaper reports, interview those who would talk to us, and maybe even provide Jerry Carr and Special Crimes with new leads."

My blood started forming ice crystals as it sluggishly circulated through my body.

"And I nominate the Gorman murder for our first investigation," said Megan. "As Ryan said in his lecture, the young grandson was suspected but never arrested, and he finally committed suicide a year later, still claiming his innocence. In fact, no one was ever formally charged with the crime."

That did it! "The Gorman murder was only twenty years ago, Megan. The Gorman family still lives in Amarillo, still owns Gorman Oil Company and Gorman Land and Cattle Company. I don't think the Gormans would appreciate your nosing into their personal tragedy.

Besides, if the young husband of the victim isn't the guilty party, then there's still a killer loose. It's one thing to point out the Gorman mansion on a mystery tour and give the audience the facts, it's quite another to knock on the door and introduce yourself as the friendly neighborhood sleuth who's going to solve their crime for them."

I was on my feet leaning over her, and I didn't even realize I had gotten off the couch. Maybe I wasn't in such bad shape after all. "Have you thought at all about how dangerous investigating a recent—and twenty years is recent—murder might be? Of course, you haven't. Just like you didn't consider it when you got involved in those other two investigations. But think a minute, Megan. Haven't you ever heard of the old saying: Let sleeping dogs lie? If there's a murderer out there, let Special Crimes wake him up. I'd rather see Jerry Carr bitten than you." I sank back on the couch and wiped my face with my sleeve. Not very civilized maybe, but every time I think of Megan investigating a murder, I break into a sweat.

She patted my knee like I was some kind of drooling old fogey. I hate it when she does that. "It's all right, Ryan. I know you worry about me, but this is an absolutely safe project. We won't be confronting the murderer—"

"How do you know that? If we start—if *you* start nosing around an old murder, and drag the rest of the club with you, how do you know you won't wake up the sleeping dog? I know you, Megan Clark." I pointed my finger at her, nearly tapping her on the nose. "And I know the rest of you." I spread my arms as though gathering them all in. "You're all nuts! You'll follow her like the rats followed the Pied Piper, and you'll end up helping her set up some risky trap to catch the murderer, just like you did the last two times. What's the old saying? Third time's the charm. Correct me if I'm wrong, but this will be the third time you busybodies have investigated a murder, and it's likely to be the charm, all right. The murderer is likely to spring the trap on *you!*"

I stopped to gauge their reactions. Rosemary and Lorene looked at me with disapproving stares, while Agnes seemed to be amused—at what I couldn't imagine. Herb Jackson looked thoughtful as he ought to, considering that he stretched the legal code of ethics every time he helped Megan set up one of her traps instead of immediately informing the police of her suspicions. Randal Anderson looked supercilious, but then, he frequently does. Megan attributes it to gas or heartburn. Candi Hobbs, Randal's significant other—bless her heart—was the only one in the circle who even remotely looked as though she was taking me seriously. She and the silver-haired man, who still hadn't introduced himself.

"Ryan, you're hysterical," said Megan with a concerned expression on her face. "Have a cup of coffee and one of Lorene's oatmeal cookies, and you'll feel better. Your glucose level is probably too low. You need a little sugar."

"I am *not* hysterical, and I don't need sugar! I'm trying to convince all of you, but particularly you, Megan, of the potential danger of constantly tempting fate. Nice, middle-class people like you can't keep dabbling in murder without eventually getting hurt. This is not one of your mystery novels. The law of averages will catch up with you." I stopped and wiped the sweat off my forehead again. It seemed I had been doing a lot of sweating lately. If I were female, I would be wondering about early menopause. But I put it down to the sheer mental effort of trying to convince Megan Elizabeth Clark, Ph.D., of her lamentable lack of judgment. That girl could teach stubborn on a graduate level.

"Ryan! We are not dabbling in murder! I don't call solving two cases involving four murders *dabbling,*" said Megan, holding her head at what I call her imperial angle, meaning she was looking down her nose at me and flaring her nostrils like Marie Antoinette just before the executioner let go of the rope on the guillotine. "If it weren't for us, the cases would be unsolved. The police certainly didn't have a clue."

Call Me Herb laughed. He's the only person I've actually heard whose laughter sounds like heh-heh-heh. "That's a wonderful play on words, Megan. The police don't have a clue. Heh-heh-heh."

Herb's statement goes a long way toward explaining why his work in progress puts everyone to sleep.

"The only reason I went along with this tour idea— other than that it might help Agnes stave off her competitors—was because all the murders happened before you were born, Megan, and there was no murderer lurking about to attack you. That, and the fact that the odds are astronomically against a white, middle-class young woman finding more than three dead bodies in the space of a year. It just can't happen again!"

I stopped and took a deep breath, let it out, and took another. I wanted sufficient oxygen in my brain to make it work at its maximum efficiency. I wasn't sure that Megan couldn't outthink me on the average day, and I wanted all my lightbulbs operating at full wattage. "However, the odds that the next dead body will be *yours,*" I said, pointing at her, "are pretty damn good if you keep playing Nancy Drew!"

I shouldn't have said that, and I knew it the minute the words left my mouth.

Megan drew herself up, her face turning red and those whiskey eyes 180 proof. "I am not Nancy Drew, and you're hovering, Ryan! I hate it when people hover over me like I'm young and stupid."

Wisely, I kept my mouth shut.

Randal stroked his goatee. "If you two keep arguing, Herb will have to ask a judge to appoint a mediator. None of us rats can do it, since we're too busy following Megan the Pied Piper."

I flinched. I hate leaving myself open to one of Randal's zingers. "I apologize. I just wanted to make you people understand that murder is not a parlor game. Someone could get hurt if you persist in playing detective, and since Megan's is the neck that is always stuck out the farthest, hers is the neck most likely to be lopped off."

"Young man, we don't *play* detective. We're very serious about investigating murder, and when you consider the cumulative number of years this group has spent solving puzzles, even if they are found between the covers of books, we have more experience than anyone in Special Crimes, including Jerry Carr. Isn't that right, Lorene?" asked Rosemary. She was still dressed in her respectable matron clothes, 1912 variety, for her part in the Boyce-Sneed scenario, and I felt like I was being lectured by my great-grandmother.

"It certainly is. And I agree with Megan. You are hovering, and young women of her generation don't appreciate being hovered over."

"Doesn't anybody understand what I'm saying? Herb, what about you? You're a lawyer. Can't you help me persuade this group not to meddle in murder?" Herb was still wearing his 1912 suit splattered with red food dye for blood. He had played Al Boyce, Jr., in Megan's scenario, and everyone, even me, agreed that no Hollywood actor could have played a better death scene than Herb.

Herb tugged on the waistcoat of his suit and sat up straighter in his chair, his face sober as a judge's. "Mind you, Ryan, I was concerned about my ethical responsibility in our first two cases, but I felt we were aiding the cause of justice rather than obstructing justice. After all, Megan had attempted to report her suspicions to Lieutenant Carr and was, as they say, brushed off. At that point, we had a civic duty to stop the murderer. I believe I could argue my case successfully in front of the bar, if anyone believed I had acted unethically."

My estimation of Herb as a lawyer went up several notches. Anyone who could tiptoe through the tulips without stepping on the petals as well as Herb just did was a hell of an attorney.

I turned to Candi Hobbs just in time to see her applaud Herb, so I didn't bother asking her opinion. She obviously was just another rat following the Piper.

"Agnes, can you at least convince this bunch to investigate a turn-of-the-century crime, so I won't have to worry about a murderer jumping out of the bushes? Better yet, how about reading up on a murder where the perpetrator is already in prison?" I heard the desperate note in my hoarse voice, but I was feeling desperate.

"What fun would there be in that, Ryan? We want a case with ambiguity, with questions left unanswered, and the Gorman case fits both criteria. What you need to do is stop trying to protect Megan. She's of the age and generation to protect herself. Although I'm sure she thinks you're sweet to try."

Agnes was a woman, at least twenty-five years older

than I, and one of my favorite people, or I might have possibly punched her out for that remark. Puppies are sweet; kittens are sweet; babies are sweet. Men are supposed to be sexy, masculine, testosterone-charged hunks. At their best they can be tender. But sweet! God, how could she call me that in front of Randal Anderson!

My last chance to make my case lay with the silver-haired stranger, who was watching us all with a thoughtful expression on his face.

"Sir, do you understand what I'm trying to say? That investigating murder is a job for the police and not for a bunch of amateur sleuths?"

The elderly man pursed his lips and looked at each of the other members, his eyes resting longest on Megan. He stood up, folded his hands over his cane, and looked at me, his blue gray eyes revealing the acuity of a much younger man. Whoever he was, and his face looked familiar, he wasn't senile or anywhere close to it.

"Dr. Stevens, isn't it?" he asked, his voice rough as Edgar G. Robinson's in *Key Largo*.

"Yes, sir, but members of Murder by the Yard generally call me Ryan—even when they would rather call me something else."

"Ryan, then. I can't support your argument, Ryan. In fact, I joined your reading group for the purpose of asking Megan Clark and Murder by the Yard to investigate the Gorman Case. You see, I'm Bruce Gorman, and it was my grandson, Randy Gorman, who committed suicide after his wife's murder."

5

"Fine, fine. All I've got to do now is find a guy called The Schemer who's about fifty, fat, smokes strong cigars, chews Chinese Dragon Liver Herb Medicine, has a scar on his shoulder, maybe."

DENNIS O'KEEFE
(undercover T man Dennis O'Brian),
T Men, 1948

"Mr. Gorman, I hope we didn't say anything to upset you," said Megan, feeling twelve years old again and caught whispering in class about the teacher. Who expected a member of the Gorman family to be sitting in the reading area of Time and Again Bookstore? Of course, she hadn't said anything she couldn't support, but then she had been able to prove everything she said about her teacher, too, and it hadn't made any difference. She still got in-school suspension for a week.

"Did you lie when you talked about the Gorman case, Dr. Clark?" asked Gorman.

"It's Megan," she said automatically. "And no, I didn't lie."

"Then you shouldn't apologize. I'm not politically correct, Megan. The truth ought to be told without adornment and without euphemism, and if someone gets their feelings hurt, so be it. You can't live in this world without your toes getting stepped on, but as it happens,

I am not offended. My grandson, Randy, was a suspect. I think he was the only suspect the police had, although they didn't say so."

The old man paused now that he had the attention of everyone in the room and wiped his lips with a crisp white handkerchief Megan would bet cost more than her entire outfit. He sat back down and laid his cane across his lap. It was wood, mahogany Megan guessed, with a curved head she suspected was gold rather than brass.

"I'm eighty-six years old, Megan, and I would like to know for certain who was responsible for my grandson's suicide before I die. I don't have time to wait for the police to solve the crime. They haven't managed to solve it in twenty years, and I don't expect them to suddenly arrest somebody now. They have given up on the case, regardless of what Lieutenant Jerry Carr might say in the paper. My grandson didn't murder Melinda, his bride, and he shot himself because he mourned her and couldn't live with the suspicion, not because he had a guilty conscience."

The old man leaned forward as if to get closer to Megan, and for a moment, she felt pinned to the couch by the intensity of his stare. "I've been reading the papers, Megan. You and this reading circle of yours are responsible for solving four murders in four months. Not only is that a one hundred percent success rate, but you do it at a damn sight faster pace than the police."

Megan swallowed and arranged her thoughts before speaking. What she was about to say was apt to offend Bruce Gorman, but he said he wanted the truth. She hoped he meant it. "Mr. Gorman, the other two cases we investigated were what you might call insider crimes. In other words, the murderer was a member of a small group we all knew. I have to believe that the Gorman case is the same. No outsider could have walked into your pool room and stolen a pool cue while four members of your family were there."

Megan saw Bruce Gorman flinch ever so slightly, and his eyes shifted away from hers for a split second before focusing on her again. "I have spent twenty years trying to convince myself of exactly the opposite, Megan. I have believed that while a member of my family may have knocked Melinda unconscious out of anger, someone else, someone outside the family, whom she had arranged to meet in the gazebo, found her and strangled her before she regained consciousness. Then my poor grandson went looking for his wife and found her dead. Isn't my scenario as likely as yours this afternoon?"

Megan pondered his suggestion for a moment. "You mean, one family member happened to wander over to the gazebo, whack Melinda on the head, drop his pool cue, and flee back to the house and whatever activity he was engaged in? Then Mr. X or Ms. X, a man or woman with whom Melinda had arranged to meet at the gazebo, finds her unconscious and strangles her for whatever reason. Then Randy Gorman goes searching for his wife, finds her dead, and sits down to mourn her. If I were an unskilled mystery writer, I might plot such an unlikely scene, but this is real life, and I don't think it happened that way. What do the rest of you think?"

Rosemary and Lorene looked at one another and shook their heads in unison. "I certainly don't remember dear Agatha using such a clumsy plot," said Rosemary, the Agatha Christie expert of Murder by the Yard.

"And certain Dorothy Sayers was more skillful than that," said Lorene. "Even her Montague Egg short stories, which are not up to the standards of Lord Peter Wimsey, are more clever than the plot you're describing,

Mr. Gorman. Candi, you've been studying mystery fiction for your master's thesis. Have you run across Mr. Gorman's plot?"

Candi blinked rapidly. She had switched from her Coke-bottle glasses to contacts after she and Randal became a duo, but she blinked more now. She reminded Megan of a slightly plump, round-faced, pedantic owl. "Any competent mystery writer wouldn't depend on three possible meetings with the victim, two of them coincidental. I think that's very weak plotting. I mean, did she ask Mr. Family Member with the pool cue to meet her in the gazebo? If so, then he's the murderer and not Randy Gorman. Otherwise, how did he know she was in the gazebo? Did he see her go there? If so, he must have either been watching the gazebo for exactly that purpose, or it was coincidental. He just happened to see Melinda go to the gazebo and decided to kill her. Or just to hit her because he's angry. But what will he do when she wakes up and tells her husband? If she asked Mr. Outsider to meet her, then how did he get the pool cue? I'm afraid the most logical explanation is one you don't believe, Mr. Gorman, that your grandson killed his wife. Don't you agree, Randal?"

Randal Anderson, professor of English at Amarillo College and pompous, but not as pompous in Megan's opinion as he was before Candi Hobbs began smoothing his irritating edges, stroked his goatee, neatly trimmed since Candi entered his life. "I have been mentally going through the literature while Megan and Candi were talking, and I can't think of a decent mystery writer clumsy enough in plotting to depend so heavily on coincidence. I can't speak for bad mystery writers since I don't read them."

"What literature are you talking about?" demanded

Ryan. "Annotated bibliographies of scientific journals and papers, or historical journals and papers? No, you're talking about mystery books! Fiction, for God's sake! You're going out hunting for a murderer, and your bibliography consists of storybooks!"

"Ryan, old boy, why don't you put a cork in it. Your Cassandra role is getting a little repetitive," said Randal.

"And just look what happened to Troy!" retorted Ryan.

"Ryan," said Agnes. "I think what Randal is trying to say is that you've warned us, but the fact is, no one is listening. And that's our right: not to listen."

"I guess it's your right to get killed, too," said Ryan, throwing up his hands, then folding his arms and glowering at everyone. Megan could practically see the smoke coming out of his ears.

Call Me Herb tugged on his vest, clasped his hands together at waist level, and looked at Bruce Gorman with earnestness. Megan thought earnestness was his best expression. She bet juries loved it, too. "As an attorney who frequently practices criminal law, I can tell you that defending your grandson with the outsider story would not be an effective defense. Not at all. It's the pool cue factor, you see. One has to explain it in some way that makes sense to the jury. Either your grandson hit her, then strangled her, or another family member did. "I'm sorry, sir, but that is my professional opinion."

"I just thought of a mystery in which several people went into the victim's room, but the victim was killed somewhere else, so I guess that doesn't count. I just thought of it because the sheriff who was searching it was knocked unconscious," said Megan.

"What mystery was that, Megan?" asked Agnes.

"*The Folsom Man Murders*. No, that's not right. It

was *The Sheriff and the Folsom Man Murders*, and Sheriff Matthews was searching the victim's room, and it turned out that nearly every character had been in that room. And they all had motives."

"I remember reading that mystery," said Agnes. "One of the other characters said the victim's room was as 'busy as a one-girl whorehouse on a Saturday night.' If we believe Mr. Gorman's scenario, the gazebo was that busy, too."

"But what motive did anyone have for murdering Melinda, Mr. Gorman? Did the police ever accuse your grandson of having a reason to kill his wife? Did they ever talk to the other family members about motive?"

Bruce Gorman shook his head. "Randy loved Melinda. He had no reason for killing her, and the police didn't have much luck making one up, either. I think they finally just said it was jealous rage because she hugged everyone before dinner. The police tried to attribute meanings that weren't there, because she not only hugged my son Paul and my other grandson Jimmy, but she hugged Paul's wife. It was merely her way of saying how glad she was to be in the family. We're a staid, stiff-necked bunch, and Melinda's vivaciousness was like a clean, cold wind blowing through my old house. My stepmother who was alive at the time, but didn't join us for dinner because of ill health, said that Melinda blew the stink out of the house.

"What did she mean by that, Mr. Gorman?" asked Megan.

Bruce Gorman smiled. "You have to understand that my stepmother was an outspoken woman. She was from a pioneer ranching family, like my father, but she never had much use for 'society.' That was her way of saying that the family needed new blood, commoner blood, that all the rarefied air we breathed as members of the upper crust was weakening the stock."

"And Melinda was a, uh, commoner?" asked Megan, uneasy with the phrase.

"I'm sorry. That's a bad word, but I was quoting my stepmother. She tended to see things in black and white. If the Gormans were the aristocrats, then Melinda was a commoner because her family was working class. Melinda was a secretary at Gorman Oil Company. That's how she met Randy. That's how we all knew her—as a secretary, and a very good one."

"But not someone to invite home to dinner?"

"Why would she want to come to dinner at my house—with just me, and I wasn't a young man then, and my very aged stepmother who had a hearing problem? What fun would that be for a young girl?"

"It was a rhetorical question."

For a moment she read regret in his eyes. "No, Megan, she would not have been on the invitation list except for the annual Christmas party I give for all my employees. Until Randy started dating her, of course. But I often did take her out to lunch. She was my personal secretary, and lunches were working lunches, except for her birthday."

"But your stepmother must have been wrong about weak stock because your family has held together in the face of Melinda's unsolved murder and your grandson's suicide, Mr. Gorman. Isn't that true?"

Bruce Gorman's eyes lost focus for a moment, and Megan was glad that whatever he was seeing inside his own mind was his alone. She wouldn't want to share the pain she saw on his face. Old pain. Twenty-year-old pain.

He blinked, and his eyes came back into focus, whatever pain he felt banished for the moment. "My family has shared my table every Sunday and holiday for the last twenty years, and in all that time Randy has never stopped haunting us. It is as if a place is set for him at the table, and we are all waiting for him to take his seat. Some nights I awaken suddenly, thinking I heard the gunshot, and I get up and pour myself a whiskey and wait for the sun to come up, because I know I won't sleep again that night. And when morning comes, I walk down that cold stone hall from my bedroom to Randy's, and wait outside the door until I have found sufficient courage to open it. I have to check, you see, to be sure that what I heard was my imagination."

He reached over and grasped Megan's hand. His was dry and cold, and Megan shivered at his touch. "Find out what's killing my family, Megan Clark. Lance the wound, and let the poison out, so one may meet retribution and the rest of us heal."

6

"What kind of dame are you?"
"The kind that watches out for herself."

MICKEY ROONEY
(Danny) and Jeanne Cagney (gold-digger
Vera Novak),
Quicksand, 1950

"Ryan?"

"Hmm?"

"Are you still mad at me?"

"I don't know what makes you say that."

"Because it takes fifteen minutes to drive from Time and Again to our homes. I am now sitting in my truck in my driveway, which is next to your driveway, and you have not said one word to me in that fifteen minutes. For that matter, you didn't speak to me the last thirty minutes we were at the bookstore. You're too old to act like a sullen teenager."

Ouch, that hurt. "What do you know about sullen teenagers?" I asked.

"I was a teaching assistant in graduate school, and they always gave me the freshman classes, I guess because I looked too young to teach sophomores. Try telling one of Daddy's little darlings that not only didn't she know the material on the exam, she couldn't write a halfway decent postcard, much less a literate answer to an essay question."

"Megan, I used to teach freshmen until I became curator of history at the museum and reduced my teaching load to two classes for seniors. I doubt there's a single variety of sullen teenager who hasn't crossed my path."

"Then you know what I'm talking about."

Unfortunately, I did, although I upheld the honor of pouting males everywhere by denying it. "I suppose from a certain perspective I might appear sullen, but I was quiet because I had nothing left to say."

She turned sideways in the seat. The moon shone in the back window and painted her profile in dark, dark burgundy and cream, the burgundy of her hair swirling against the cream of her cheek. Even in the moonlight, I could see the glimmer of her eyes and the downward tilt of her mouth. She reached over and clasped my hands between hers. Her hands are small, so it was like being held by a young girl, but I would never tell her that. Megan is a woman built to a small design. There's nothing girlish about her.

"You're angry, aren't you, because Murder by the Yard is going to investigate the Gorman case?" she asked, her voice a soft murmur inside the closed cab of the pickup.

I could smell the scent of pear blossoms and salty sweat and another undefinable scent that was sweet and musky at the same time. This was Megan after a day standing in the sun. Me, I just stank of sweaty man.

She squeezed my hand. "Earth to Ryan. Earth to Ryan. Are you with me?"

If I were ten years younger, hell, even five years younger, I'd take her up on that double entendre and demonstrate just how with her I could be. But not only am I her best friend's father, and therefore safe, at least in her mind, but at my age, wrestling around in the front seat of a pickup would probably throw my back out.

"I'm listening," I mumbled.

"Are you still mad at me and Murder by the Yard?"

I shook my head, more to wake myself from my trance than to indicate a negative. "You can't hide behind the reading club, Megan. Without you, the other members would happily spend their time arguing about the literary merits of the female sleuths in Sue Grafton, Sara Paretsky, and Marcia Muller."

"Ryan! I didn't know you even knew who Sara Paretsky or Marcia Muller were."

"Can't sleep through every meeting, Angel. But don't change the subject, which is your leadership of Murder by the Yard. Without you, none of those folks would even think of actually investigating a murder as opposed to sitting around and talking about it. Doesn't it worry you that you're responsible for those people putting themselves at risk?"

I saw her scrape her teeth over her lower lip. She always does that when's she nervous—or else she chews her thumbnail. "Of course I worry about it, Ryan. What kind of person do you think I am? That's why I always take the risks. You notice that I use the others as lookouts or hidden witnesses, but never have I asked anyone else to confront a murderer. That's my responsibility, and I know how to watch out for myself."

"There's always a first time, Megan, and that's what I'm afraid of now. If Randy Gorman didn't kill his wife, then somebody has gotten away with murder for twenty years! Do you think he—or she—will allow you to upset his—or her—apple cart?"

"Just say he, Ryan. Statistically, few stranglers of adults are women."

"Well, *he* might try to strangle *you*."

"I'm not going to confront the murderer. I—*we*—are just going to do an investigation and turn over the results to Bruce Gorman. Let him confront the murderer. After all, it'll be a member of his own family. And admit it, weren't you touched by Bruce Gorman's story? Now that he's a member of Murder by the Yard, we have to help him."

"I believe his story, and I wouldn't want to have lived my last twenty years in that kind of hell, but he knew his words were like waving a red flag in front of a bull, the red flag being an invitation to dabble in murder, and the bull being you. And I also noticed something else. All of us said "call me Ryan" or "call me Megan" or "call me Agnes," but I never heard Bruce Gorman say "call me Bruce." He joined Murder by the Yard so you would help him. He hired you for the price of filling out a questionnaire. Why else do you think he asked you all those questions at each of the murder sites? He was interviewing you without your realizing it. You're hired help, Megan, and believe me, he'll expect his money's worth just as if he paid you a big retainer."

She shook her head at my words, and I wanted to shake her in frustration. "Ryan, I wanted to study the Gorman case before I knew who that white-haired old man was. And I know he tried to manipulate me, but how can you manipulate somebody who is in agreement with you? Besides, I sympathize with him. In his place, I would do just about anything to avoid waking up over and over again to the sound of the gunshot that took my grandson's life. Imagine twenty years worth of nights like that! In his place, I would make a pact with the devil for a peaceful night. But he didn't have to do that. All he had to do was persuade me to take the case, and I was an easy mark, whether he knew it or not. Just as Agnes is still touched by the Boyce-Sneed case and Rosemary remembers the Thornton case, I remember the Gorman Case. I was only six, but I remember the fear. My mother wouldn't let me out of her sight for weeks. Don't you remember her walking me over to your house to play with Evin? My mother didn't know if Randy Gorman murdered his wife or if some monster was loose in the neighborhood, and the Gorman mansion is just six blocks down the street from us. Monsters are very real when you're six. Then, of course, Randy Gorman committed suicide, and everyone breathed easier. But I always wondered if he was guilty because I was so young and couldn't imagine that a man would kill his wife. I guess I felt that way because my father died the year before the murder, and I missed him so much. And now I'll finally know if the young husband is really innocent. I know his grandfather believes he is, but grandfathers are frequently biased."

I let out my breath in a sigh. I didn't know the Gorman case ever touched her, an only child from a middle-class home with no ties to the Gormans. I never imagined that Randy Gorman and her father were intertwined in her memory. Certain psychiatrists say there is a child within us. Maybe they were right. Maybe whenever Megan thought of the Gorman murder, she was six years old again. She knew her father would never hurt her mother, but the accusations against Randy Gorman confused her and made her unsure of her own convictions. Maybe I was indulging in psychobabble, but maybe I wasn't. Maybe Megan the child was the reason behind why Megan the woman was so determined to investigate the Gorman case. If that was so, then nothing I said would change her mind. But I had to try.

"I suppose it won't do any good to remind you again of sleeping dogs and the waking thereof."

She leaned over and kissed my cheek. "Not a bit."

The next day was Friday, and I had to teach my two classes, then clear up some paperwork at the museum, so it was well past noon before I walked through Megan's front door. Her adopted beagle, Rembrandt, met me, voicing in a deep baritone his usual displeasure at my appearance. I concluded long ago that Rembrandt sensed my interest in his mistress, decided that I was a potential rival to her affections, and took every opportunity short of biting to annoy me. I am not attributing human intelligence and characteristics to him. I don't need to. Any dog intelligent enough to curl his lip up to expose a fine set of teeth but only do it when his goddess isn't in the room and I am, doesn't need any extra IQ. He's smart enough as he is.

"Ryan, I'm in the kitchen."

"Shall we go to the kitchen, Rembrandt?" I asked.

The dog curled his lip over his teeth, and for a beagle, he had a fine set of long, sharp teeth, gave voice to one last deep howl, then waddled toward the kitchen. Did I mention that Rembrandt is fifteen years old, built like a beer keg on legs, and has survived all manner of doggy illnesses, including testicular cancer? As I followed him, it occurred to me for the first time that he might dislike me for an entirely different reason. I had balls and he didn't.

The first person I saw was Herb Jackson in his three-piece lawyer suit. The woman sitting across from him was a sturdy, buxom, prematurely gray-haired lady of some indeterminate age, wearing a severe black suit with a blouse that hugged her throat and a black skirt that reached midcalf, an unattractive length on any woman, in my opinion. Her dark brown eyes peered at me through large horn-rimmed glasses with square lenses tinted a medium beige. Her skin was sallow with too much pink blush, and her eyebrows met over her nose. Unfortunately, her hands gave her away and so did her dog. Rembrandt immediately reared up as gracefully as a beer keg on legs could and put his head in the woman's lap.

"It's not Halloween. What are you dressed up for, Megan?" I asked and watched, amazed, as she spat out enough cotton balls to fill a coffee cup and took off her glasses.

"What gave me away?"

"Your hands. You'd better wear gloves. And it would help if you caged up Rembrandt."

"No one wears gloves, Ryan, unless it's winter, and a hardworking secretary taking down notes certainly wouldn't. I'll have to use the same shade of makeup I'm wearing on my face on my hands and hope Jerry doesn't notice any similarities between Herb's secretary, Miss Vassar, and Megan Clark."

I felt my heart rate pick up, a common occurrence when I catch Megan in the middle of one of her nefarious schemes. "By Jerry, do you mean Lieutenant Jerry Carr of Special Crimes?"

Her fingers tapped the top of the table, a sign of impatience, boredom, or another scheme. "I don't know any other Jerry."

I turned my attention to Herb, who was squirming as if his chair was red hot and glancing around the kitchen to avoid eye contact. "Just what part do you play in

Megan's little scenario, Mr. Herbert Jackson the Third, and I say 'Megan's scenario' because her sense of drama has been locked on automatic ever since she first came up with the idea of a murder tour—which, if you recall, I thought was a bad idea from the get go—so I find you innocent of planning whatever idiocy you two are involved in but guilty of going along with it. I can almost hear the notes of the Pied Piper's flute." I pulled out a chair, turned it around, and sat down, my arms resting on its back. "Now, which one of you is going to tell me exactly what this idiocy is all about."

Megan's eyes, whiskey colored again now that she had taken off the tinted glasses, avoided mine, and her glance skittered around the kitchen, bouncing off the cabinets and appliances before finally resting on the salt and pepper shakers sitting in the middle of the table. I knew she must be feeling uneasy about her plan, whatever it was, because otherwise she would have stared me down. I don't often have the advantage of her, and I was not only enjoying it, but I planned to push her farther into the corner.

With all the talk of the Pied Piper and rats, I should have remembered that a cornered rat always fights.

Megan's eyes finally met mine. "This is not idiocy, Ryan. Bruce Gorman hired Herb this morning for a nominal retainer, so we could go talk to Jerry Carr about the case. Since no one was ever arrested and prosecuted, the only public document we can see is the autopsy report, so Herb and I came up with this idea of representing the family, who are concerned that the Melinda Gorman murder case is gathering dust in some file cabinet. If we're lucky, Jerry may tell us all or most of the information in the file. Being able to read everyone's statement would be ideal, as well as looking at the other documents, but we'll take what we can get. But we wouldn't get anything at all if I went in Jerry's office as myself. You know how sensitive he is since I—and Murder by the Yard—have solved four murders. He isn't required by law to talk to us. And by the way, I don't appreciate your prejudging my plan."

I held up my hands. "Hey, prejudgment always gets a bad rap, but if I know the people involved in a certain situation—and I do—then I can anticipate the consequences whether good or bad, and in this case, bad. Your disguise will not fool Jerry Carr for a minute, and he will throw you and Herb out of his office if he doesn't throw you in jail. I think Herb is safe from the pokey if he really has paper proof that Gorman hired him—"

"I have a copy of our agreement," said Herb. "Actually, I have three copies: one for my file, one for the general office files, and one for the bookkeeper. I left Mr. Gorman's copy with him, of course."

Why did I know that anything Herb did would be in triplicate at least? "If I were you, I'd hang on to those copies like they were a signed first edition of *Murder on the Orient Express*. In fact, I would show Jerry Carr a copy before I started asking questions. It would throw him off balance for one of the Murder by the Yard groupies to actually have a legitimate reason to be poking his nose in murder. Of course, your legitimacy will be called into question when 'Miss Vassar' here is fingerprinted and has her mug shot taken."

"There is nothing illegal about impersonating an imaginary secretary," said Megan.

Her calm was beginning to worry me. Usually, when's she caught doing something she shouldn't do, she goes on the offensive, but this rat hadn't offered to bite me yet.

"I'm sure that Jerry Carr will think of something, but at the very least, he will throw you out."

Herb cleared his throat and laid his agreement in front of me, pointing to a line with a well-manicured fingernail. Rough cuticles and Herbert Jackson III are an oxymoron. "Technically, Lieutenant Carr will not be able to harass Megan for any reason. If you will read section A of this agreement, it says, "The said Herbert Jackson III and such of his employees as he deems necessary will represent Bruce Gorman in the matter of the murder of Melinda Gorman." Herb looked up at me and tugged on his vest. "I have employed Megan Clark, a.k.a. Violet Vassar, as a personal assistant. There is a written employment agreement in triplicate with both her real name and her alias, so we are operating within the letter of the law."

Megan looked too smug for her own good.

"We won't talk about the spirit of the law for the moment," I said. "But tell me, Miss Pris, why Herb can't talk to Jerry by himself? Why do you have to go along in disguise?"

Megan narrowed her eyes. The Miss Pris hadn't set well with her. I supposed I would pay for it later.

"Oh, it's out of the question for me to go by myself," said Herb, looking horrified at the idea. "I'm not as experienced at solving puzzles as Megan or the other members of Murder by the Yard. All those thousands and thousands of mysteries have given them a keen eye for detail and for what questions to ask. And Megan's training as a paleopathologist and archaeologist, together with her familiarity with mysteries, make her the leader in interrogation. But, as she told you, Jerry Carr would probably be hesitant to talk to her even though she has the confidence of the Gorman family. The lieutenant tends to underestimate our Megan."

That was true. He tended to underestimate the trouble she could create for herself.

"At any rate," continued Herb. "Megan and I decided that she would accompany me as my secretary, and she could slip me notes as to questions to ask as my conversation with Lieutenant Carr progresses."

"So you're playing dress up, Megan," I said.

"I am going in *disguise*," she retorted, icicles hanging from every syllable. "If you recall, I wore a disguise once during our first murder investigation, and we learned some valuable facts as a result. Also, if you recall, your favorite detective, Kinsey Millhone, often wears disguises."

"Right now, you remind me of Lucy Ricardo. She wore disguises and she had red hair, too." Maybe that was a cheap shot, but I was getting desperate.

Megan sighed and rolled her eyes toward the ceiling. I had seen my oldest daughter do exactly that same thing whenever she decided talking to dear old Dad was a waste of time. But I wasn't Megan's dad, and my feelings for her were far from fatherly.

"We were going to ask you to come with us, Ryan, but with your attitude, you'd probably ruin the whole interview." Her voice got more and more muffled as she stuck one cotton ball after another in her mouth, until her face was moon shaped.

She stood up, and I looked up at her. She stood at least three inches taller than her normal five feet two if she stretched. "What have you done to yourself?"

"Lifts in my shoes," she lisped, the cotton in her mouth interfering with her diction.

She leaned over and kissed me on the lips. It wasn't

a deep, tongue-swirling kind of kiss, but it wasn't any peck either. If I had been Rembrandt, I would have rolled over for a tummy rub.

"Be careful," I said when I finally got my breath back. "I'll wait in the car."

7

"How did you get past the NO VISITORS sign?"
"I walked straight past it."

ROBERT YOUNG
(architect Jeff Cohalan) and Betsy Drake (his
girlfriend Ellen Foster),
The Second Woman, 1950

"So old man Gorman hired you?" asked Lieutenant Jerry Carr.

Megan kept her eyes on her employer, Call Me Herb, to avoid looking at Jerry. Her tinted glasses might turn her pale brown eyes dark, but she doubted that she could carry off the masquerade if she had to look Jerry in the eye. She didn't rate her acting skills all that highly, despite doing Shakespeare in the park every summer. It was one thing to play Queen Elizabeth in *Richard III* in front of an audience of mostly strangers; it was another to play Violet Vassar to an audience of one, that one being Jerry Carr, who knew her. Maybe not in the biblical sense, but he knew her, nonetheless. Fortunately, he had barely glanced at her when Herb introduced her. Of course, looking middle-aged and plain and dressed in dowdy clothes was one way to guarantee not to get a second look from a man unless he was fat, over sixty, and had crooked teeth. In her present disguise, even the little old men who spent most of their days in the reference department at the library wouldn't hit on her. Still, it was a tiny blow to her self-esteem that Jerry hadn't seen beneath her disguise. Ryan had recognized her immediately. He did have the advantage of seeing her in her own kitchen, and Rembrandt had laid his head in her lap, but Megan had a premonition that Ryan would recognize her if they were in a pitch-black room and he was wearing a blindfold. She wasn't sure what that said about Ryan, and she didn't have time to think about it now. She'd think about it tomorrow.

"Mr. Gorman has retained me to look into the progress made in the Melinda Gorman murder case," said Herb. "It has been twenty years, after all, and as Mr. Gorman is quite elderly, he wants some kind of resolution to the case. He is of that age, Lieutenant, when he wants closure on unsettled issues, and the murder of Melinda Gorman is the most pressing issue in his life."

Megan looked at Jerry from underneath her lashes. He was twirling a pencil between his palms and looking thoughtful. Herb was putting on a terrific act, but she wasn't sure Jerry was buying it.

"Gorman has a whole firm of attorneys on retainer. How come he hired you, Jackson?

"Mr. Gorman took the murder tour sponsored by Murder by the Yard. Given the recent success in solving murders enjoyed by our little circle, I believe he thought I was a good choice to, well, to be blunt, to investigate the investigation."

Jerry snapped the pencil in two when Herb mentioned Murder by the Yard, and Megan flinched. It was definitely a good thing she had not come as herself. Jerry was very, very sensitive about the reading circle. Herb, however, had not indicated in any way that he noticed Jerry's agitation. Not for the first time, Megan thought

Herb had taken up the wrong profession. He should have gone into acting.

"So Gorman is unhappy with the police investigation," said Jerry. "He might be even more unhappy when you tell him the results of your visit." He turned around in his chair and lifted two large cardboard boxes onto his desk. "These boxes are the result of a year's investigation. After you called this morning, I pulled them off the shelves and looked over the papers—as we do at least once a year. No case is closed until there is an arrest and conviction, Jackson."

Megan scribbled on a notepad and passed a question to Herb. He rubbed the back of his neck while he read the note as unobtrusively as possible. "What about Mr. Randy Gorman's suicide, Lieutenant Carr? Didn't that in effect close the case as far as the police were concerned?"

Jerry folded his hands and rested them on top of his desk. Megan noticed that his knuckles were white from his grip. For some reason, their questions were disturbing Jerry, and she wondered why.

"The case was at a standstill before the suicide, and you're right to an extent; lots of people wanted the case closed at that point. It was a nice, neat ending: Randy Gorman shot himself after being suspected of his wife's murder. The problem is that Randy Gorman was no more a suspect than several other members of the family. Yeah, the police concentrated on him at first, even gave him the Miranda warning each time before they questioned him, so he would know he was a suspect. Just in case he confessed, you know, he couldn't claim he hadn't been given his rights. But toward the end of that first year, if you looked at the case objectively—which I have, because I wasn't a cop twenty years ago, I wasn't even out of junior high—the police had eight, maybe ten people who could have killed Melinda Gorman. I'll give you some advice to pass along to old man Gorman, Jackson. Tell him to leave it alone, or he'll be sitting at his dinner table wondering which of his family murdered Melinda and let Randy take the fall for it. Because that's what he did by sticking that gun in his mouth, he took the fall for the whole family."

"Could you be more specific, Lieutenant?" asked Herb. "Which eight or ten people could have murdered Melinda?"

"The whole damn clan, Jackson, from old man Gorman down to the teenage grandson, because sure as hell somebody in that family did the deed, and I don't necessarily believe Randy Gorman was that somebody. Maybe he was, maybe he wasn't. The cops weren't sure twenty years ago. Lieutenant Roberts—you ever work with the lieutenant, Jackson?"

Herb nodded. "I was just starting out in the legal profession when I received a court appointment to represent this young man—hardly more than a boy—for stealing a money order. Despite his claim that he was being framed, I was ready to recommend to the boy that he plead guilty in return for a lesser sentence, when Lieutenant Roberts stopped me in the hall outside the courtroom. He asked me if I thought it was odd that the defendant's fingerprints were found on the money order only once. If the boy had stolen the money order from his landlady's purse, folded it up, and put it in his billfold, as the creases on the money order clearly showed was done, then removed it from the billfold and put it in the glove compartment of his car, wouldn't I expect to find more fingerprints? I presented that argument to the jury, and they acquitted my client. Lieutenant Roberts was not the arresting officer and had only heard about the case secondhand after the boy had been indicted, but from the evidence, he didn't believe the boy was guilty, so he told the rookie attorney how to win the case. I've always believed that if there was a hall of fame for police officers, Lieutenant Roberts should be the first one elected."

"I never met him, but I heard enough about him to believe I missed knowing a good man and a good cop," said Jerry. "He retired the day after Randy Gorman killed himself."

Megan heard a fly buzzing in the silence that followed Jerry's last abrupt statement. Questions buzzed in her head almost as loudly. She scribbled several down on her notepad, tore off the page, and handed it to Herb. He glanced at the questions and cleared his throat. "Why did Lieutenant Roberts resign?"

"I don't know. Like I said, I never knew the man, but if I was guessing—and I'm only guessing—I think he blamed himself for Gorman's suicide. Maybe he thought he should have already made an arrest, but I've looked at the Gormans' statements, and I don't see how Roberts could have done anything differently. Looking at it objectively, the rest of the Gormans could have been guilty or they could've been innocent. If you want to nitpick, none of them had alibis worth spit. If Randy Gorman hadn't been found by his wife's body, he wouldn't have gotten much more attention than the rest. His fingerprints were on the cue stick, but his fingerprints were on all the cue sticks. It turned out that he polished the cue sticks that afternoon, so the police couldn't say absolutely that his fingerprints proved he whacked his wife of three weeks in the head. And there was no motive. The state says we don't have to prove motive, but the prosecutors damn near insist on a motive they can argue to a jury. Juries want to know why one person kills another. Even if both parties are scumbags, and I'm not saying the Gormans are, juries still want to know the motive. And Roberts tried hard to find a motive. I know, I've read his reports."

Silence descended again and stretched out. Megan could feel Jerry's eyes on her, and she glanced up to see him studying her, a puzzled look on his face. She bent her head over her notepad and kicked Herb's shin. He winced, which she hoped Jerry Carr hadn't seen, and quickly asked another question. "May we read Lieutenant Roberts's reports and also the Gormans' statements?"

Jerry whirled around in his chair and looked out the narrow window in his small office. Not more than nine feet by nine feet, with a desk, office chair, two filing cabinets, and two molded plastic chairs for visitors, Jerry's office would give most men an attack of claustrophobia. Certainly it gave Megan a nervous stomach, but that might be the consequence of her previous visits, all of which resulted in Jerry Carr's warning her to keep her nose out of Special Crimes' business. She had never considered herself a rebel exactly but rather an independent, self-reliant woman who would defy authority if she believed authority was wrong. She supposed it was her upbringing. Anyone whose mother would demonstrate and on occasion go to jail in support of a cause she believed right could hardly be expected to have a follow-the-leader personality. Still, unlike her mother, she didn't go out of her way to spit in the eye of authority. For instance, she would have preferred to discuss the Gorman case with Jerry minus the disguise, but as long as he refused to admit that her training in archaeology and paleopathology qualified her to work with the police whenever she happened to discover a murder victim, then she would do what she had to do. Jerry Carr's refusal to make her at least a consultant to Special Crimes was ridiculous, in view of her training. If she was a man, or at least six inches taller and plain, she bet they would be consulting right now. Being short and cute and having dated Jerry Carr—until he suspected her of murder—constituted three handicaps she couldn't overcome.

When the silence following Herb's question stretched out until Megan considered throwing something at the back of Jerry Carr's head, he turned around, folded his hands, and rested them on his desk. "The Gorman case is still open; therefore, the reports and statements, evidence lists, etc., are not public documents, so I don't have to make them available to you. And I won't. In my opinion, someone who was in that house the night of September eighteen murdered Melinda Gorman. Since I don't know which Gorman is the guilty one, I'm not making available to a suspect every damn fact the police know."

Herb nodded and was silent for a moment before leaning closer to Jerry's desk. "Lieutenant Carr, I understand your position, and I sympathize with it, but I'm afraid your noncooperation will not do. Not at all. I want to make clear to you that Mr. Gorman is prepared to go to great lengths to, uh, jump-start this investigation."

"One of the great lengths being to hire you and that busybody reading circle, particularly Megan Clark, to find the murderer," said Jerry. "I want to warn you, and please pass this along to Megan, that I will arrest any of you for obstruction of justice if I catch you taking any overt action in the matter of the murder of Melinda Gorman. Is that clear enough, Mr. Jackson?"

"Perfectly clear, Lieutenant, and I'm sure you will make it equally clear during the press conference Mr. Gorman will be giving. I doubt your point of view will receive the attention it deserves once it is known that the Panhandle's own Nancy Drew, Megan Clark, aided by her assistants, the other members of the reading circle, will be investigating the Gorman case. Megan is a, uh, hot topic at present. I understand all the local stations had higher numbers of viewers during the murder tour. I also understand that the newspaper sold out its edition about the tour. I'm sure all the media will be anxious to interview her. I can't say the same about you."

Megan watched Jerry's face turn puce. She hoped he didn't have hypertension, but she supposed he was a little young for that. She glanced at Herb, sitting calmly in his chair with his hands folded and resting on his crossed legs. She was seeing all kinds of different sides to Herbert Jackson III, and she felt his present performance deserved a standing ovation. Except for the Nancy Drew remark. She would have to talk to Herb about that.

Jerry drew in several deep breaths that whistled through his clenched teeth before he finally spoke in a voice that sounded like he was strangling every syllable. "Perhaps we can compromise, but I want you to know that I am doing so under duress, and there are certain facts I *will not* give you, no matter how many press conferences you call."

"I'm certain that Mr. Gorman will understand your position, and I hope you understand his," said Herb. "Miss Vassar, if you would take this down, please. Go ahead, Lieutenant."

"There were eleven people at dinner in the Gorman mansion that night, including Melinda Gorman. Bruce

Gorman invited the clan, plus Melinda's brother and mom. After dinner, Melinda goes upstairs to hers and Randy Gorman's room. Randy's youngest brother, Jimmy, a teenager with a hot date after dinner, also supposedly leaves, but no one admits to hearing his car or knowing if he stopped by the rec room for a pool cue on his way out the door. After dinner, Randy Gorman, his cousin Jake, his father Paul, and Melinda's brother, Tommy Mitchell, were playing pool. All left the room at some time during the games. In the living room, or sitting room, or parlor, or whatever you call the room next to the dinning room, are Melinda's mom, Janice Mitchell, Bruce Gorman, his grandson, Trent, and Michele, Randy's mother, all peacefully playing bridge. Deanne, Randy Gorman's sister-in-law and Trent Gorman's wife, was quietly reading a book in the library. Not only does that house have a library nearly as big as the fiction department at the downtown branch of the public library, but it looks as if the books have been read. Anyway, she was reading, or so she said. No witnesses, no real alibi. For that matter, nobody had a real alibi. For example, anybody in that bridge game could have waltzed out to the gazebo while she or he was dummy, and dispatched the bride to the hereafter."

Megan scribbled a note to Herb. "What about the cue stick?" he asked.

Jerry Carr frowned at the interruption. Megan thought it was as if he wanted to spit out all the information he had decided to divulge as quickly as possible and get it over with. "The cue sticks were in a cabinet on the wall beside the door to the rec room. Anyone could have reached in and grabbed a stick without being noticed if he—or she—was careful. Of course, nothing says a cue stick wasn't hidden someplace in the house before dinner. Damn thing is big as a castle. A pair of gloves to prevent the killer from leaving his prints, a dash across the lawn to the gazebo, a quick whack, an equally quick strangulation, and the killer is back dealing cards for another hand of bridge or racking up balls for another game of pool. The main reason the investigation focused on Randy Gorman early was his fingerprints were on the cue stick, and he was found with the body, which the idiot admitting moving, so he could put a cushion under her head. So Lieutenant Roberts had the husband—who is always the first to be suspected when his wife is murdered—with blood on his hands and his fingerprints on the cue stick. Anybody but Roberts probably would have arrested Randy Gorman five minutes after reaching the crime scene, but Roberts always gave suspects and evidence a second look. He gave Randy Gorman a third and fourth look and concluded that he wasn't any more likely to have killed his wife than anyone else in the Gorman house that night, even though he looked guilty. Roberts always looked beyond appearances."

Herb glanced down at another of Megan's scribbled questions. "Did Roberts suspect one member of the family over the others?"

"Not according to his notes."

"Surely he didn't suspect Melinda's mother?"

Jerry Carr picked up a paper clip and began to straighten it. Megan wondered why he didn't answer immediately. Finally, he looked up. "Lieutenant Roberts had been a cop for thirty years; I've been one for twelve. I'm betting he investigated at least a few mama guppy cases. I certainly have."

"Mama guppy?" asked Herb.

"Mama guppies devour their young if you don't separate the babies from them. Some human mamas do the same thing. But Lieutenant Roberts didn't mention suspecting Janice Mitchell any more than anyone else. Not according to his written reports, anyway."

"What about his field notebook? Did he leave that or take it with him when he retired?" asked Megan, then cringed. She might be able to disguise her physical appearance, but her voice was unmistakable: a light, sweet, second soprano, very distinct despite all the cotton balls in her mouth.

She thought Jerry Carr might suffer whiplash, so fast did he turn his head to glare at her. "I thought there was something familiar about you. I should have listened to my intuition. Megan, get out of my office and take your tame lawyer with you. Damn it, but I can't believe I fell for this."

Megan pulled off her wig. It itched, and besides, the cat was already out of the bag and scratching the couch, so to speak. "That's the kind of attitude that made me come in disguise, Jerry! You didn't fall for anything. Mr. Gorman asked Murder by the Yard to look into the case, and as a lawyer, Herb can represent the family and hire the rest of us as research assistants. We all have employment contracts to prove it. There is precedence for the police allowing an outsider to examine the evidence and statements; specifically the A. D. Payne case, when Gene Howe, the newspaper editor, called in A. B. MacDonald, a reporter for the *Kansas City Star*, to aid the police. In fact, it was A. B. MacDonald who was actually responsible for solving the case."

Jerry stood up and leaned over his desk until his face was only inches from Megan's. "That was *seventy* years ago, and it was a different time and a different police department."

"Yes!" exclaimed Megan. "A police department not too proud to accept help from amateurs."

"I don't care if God himself appointed you to this task, if you do anything—*anything!*—to interfere with this investigation, I will toss you in jail, and I don't care if my mother will refuse to speak to me for 'harassing that cute little librarian.' If my mother knew you the way I do, she wouldn't think you were so cute."

"Want to bet, Jerry?" asked Megan. "Guess who went along on the murder tour and is thinking of joining Murder by the Yard?"

Jerry sat down in his chair and grabbed handfuls of hair. "Just get your Nancy Drew act out of here, Megan, before I say something I'll have to apologize for later." He looked up at the ceiling. "God, why me? What did I ever do to deserve Megan Clark?"

"If it weren't you, it would be someone else, Jerry, and by the way, I'm *not* Nancy Drew."

He pointed toward the door. "Out!"

Megan figured she had pushed about as far as she dared, so she rose and sauntered out, followed by a worried-looking Herb.

"We may have gone too far, Megan," said Herb as he followed her down the long hallway. "I mean, we don't want to interfere with a police investigation or obstruct justice. At least, I don't. The bar association takes a dim view of those sorts of things."

"Don't worry, Herb. You have your retainer agreement, so you're covered. As for me, I don't see how I can interfere in a nonexistent investigation. You heard Jerry. Special Crimes looks over the case once a year. That's not an investigation; that's an inventory."

LOVE OR MONEY: THE A. D. PAYNE CASE

"On June 27, 1930, young Mrs. Eva Payne and her 11-year-old son, Arthur Payne, Jr., got in the family's Durant coach to drive from the Payne's trim little bungalow at 3711 Fountain Terrace to downtown Amarillo. The family planned to leave on vacation the next day and Eva Payne had errands to run. As she was just learning to drive, her husband, Arthur Payne, backed the car into the garage, so his wife wouldn't have to worry about reverse gears. As she and her son turned onto Line Avenue, young Arthur Junior told his mother he smelled something burning. Eva Payne speeded up, thinking that the smell would go away, and for a moment it did, then returned, a acrid order warning of something wrong. At that moment the car exploded, killing Eva Payne instantly and injuring young Arthur. The burning hulk came to rest in front of an alley between Mississippi and Louisana Streets. Sheriff William N. Thompson, Chief of Police W. R. McDowell, Chief of Detectives M. M. Scott, and District Attorney Edward W. Thomerson arrived at the crime scene, ordered Mrs. Payne's body be taken to the morgue and her son to the hospital, and began to try to decide the cause of the explosion. Witnesses said the car blew apart from the inside. A time bomb. Murder. But how was it done and who would have wanted to kill Eva Payne, an ordinary wife and mother going about her business? The real target must have been her husband, A. D. Payne, who most often drove the car. But investigators found no enemies of the young attorney, and they still didn't know how the explosion happened other than young Arthur claimed he smelled a dynamite fuse burning. He had smelled one before and recognized the smell. Then a anonymous letter arrived addressed to Police, Amarillo, Tex. It told a story of explosives from the site of an unfinished hotel being put in the wrong car, and its owner driving off before the mistake could be rectified. At first the police accepted the letter at face value, then became suspicious, but the investigation was at a standstill. At this point, Gene Howe, editor of the *Amarillo News and Globe*, wrote to an investigative reporter, A. B. MacDonald of the *Kansas City Star*, suggesting he look into the case. It is MacDonald who points out the obvious: the only person who gains from Eva Payne's death is her husband, A. D. Payne, who holds a double indemnity insurance policy on his wife—and his son. The amounts are trivial in today's terms—thirty thousand dollars altogether—but that was a much more substantial amount in 1930 dollars. Then another motive appears: an attractive former secretary who confesses to MacDonald and the police that Payne had fallen in love with her and promised to get a divorce. When Payne is arrested, police find a carbon copy of the anonymous letter in his pocket. Despite that, as an attorney Payne knew that convicting him would be difficult, if not impossible, but in another of the twists the case is known for, A. D. Payne confesses. Sure now of a conviction, the District Attorney and the police are relieved to have solved the case, and can turn their attention to calm the city's lynch fever. But another twist awaits. On August 30th, at 12: 21 A.M., a blast rips through the Potter County jail as

A. D. Payne takes the explosive way out of his dilemma. One of his cell mates, R. L. Conder, Jr., states that Payne had worn a three-inch long vial of powder taken from a stick of dynamite taped between his legs and tight against his body where repeated searches failed to discover it. A firecracker fuse was inserted into the bottle and the bottle sealed with putty. Once Payne was ready to die, he ripped the bottle loose, lit the fuse with a lighted cigarette, and rolled over holding the bottle between his chest and the mattress of his bunk. The explosion ripped open his chest and abdomen. In a press conference, Sheriff Bill Thompson said Payne was searched after every jail visit, but couldn't say whether or not the defendant had ever removed his underwear or trousers.

Dr. Ryan Stevens on the circumstances of the A. D. Payne case, June 27 to August 30, 1930.

"The sooner I am lowered into a grave, the better it will be for all concerned," I told the police. They took it for remorse, but they did not understand. As I told my former law partner, James O. Cade, I did not murder my wife. I merely removed her. I feared I was going mad and did not want her to see me in such a state, and since insanity was in the male line, I plotted to kill my son, so he would not suffer disgrace. But she would not die! For six months I had tried to rid myself of my wife, but failed. The first time I tried to maneuver our car in front of a train with her in it. The second time I tricked her into taking an overdose of sleeping pills, but the infernal woman only got sick to her stomach. The third time I inserted a gas pipe into our bedroom while she was sleeping and let the gas flow for several hours. She only

got a headache. The fourth time I took her driving around a nearby lake, hoping for an opportunity to drown her, but no such opportunity arose. Besides, I didn't know that I possess the cruelty to have thrust her beneath the water, my college sweetheart. Finally, I rigged a loaded shotgun in our closet with one end of a string attached to the trigger and the other end attached to the door, so whoever opened it would receive the blast. Then I asked her to get me my bathrobe out of the closet. She did, the gun fired, but she only received a wound above the wrist. The woman led a charmed life! I could not remove her! In desperation, I thought of the family car. I obtained three sticks of dynamite and put them behind the front seat, hidden by a bag of feed. I capped the dynamite, ran the fuse under the floorboard and attached it to the exhaust pipe. Then I made a spirit lamp out of an oil can, toweling, and alcohol and wired it to the universal joint. When the driver released the hand brake, the movement brought the dynamite fuse to the spirit lamp. On June 27th, I lit the spirit lamp, and taking my daughter, Bobbie Jean, by the hand, we walked the three miles to my office. This time my plan worked perfectly except that the gas tank did not catch on fire and obliterate all traces of the dynamite. My son also lived although scarred for life.

"I hate newspaper men. That interfering editor of the paper, Gene Howe, called in another of his breed, a certain A. B. MacDonald of the Kansas City Star. MacDonald looked over the case and claimed I was the only one to gain from my wife's death. Then he tracked down my former secretary who spilled the beans about my feelings toward her. One cannot trust a woman. First my wife refuses for months to die, then Verona "confesses" to the police.

"Cade wants me to plead insanity at my trial. I will not do it."

"I can always cheat the chair. I can go anytime I want to."

"Once Verona talked I knew the police would be after me, so I prepared for the moment. I poured the powder from a stick of dynamite into a three-inch bottle about the thickness of a lead pencil. I taped it between my legs, up high against my body where I knew the police would never find it. I may be charged with murder, but I am not a common thug. The police will not search my underwear. The district attorney, Edward W. Thomerson, sat in my cell in Stinnett where I was first arrested, and watched me shave and dress. All the time the bottle was taped between my legs under my summer underwear. If only Gene Howe had kept his nose out of my business, I would not be in this fix.

"I saw my children today—at least Ladell and Arthur Junior. He seems to have forgiven me. I am leaving behind another diary that they may read. In it I told them to grow up to be decent men and women and to forget their daddy, but to always remember that they were born of love and affection between their mother and daddy. I also asked to be buried beside my dear wife Eva. Strange that I was unable to accomplish anything in the way of business once she was gone. I feel useless without her. I had not expected that.

"As I wrote in the other diary, the one I will give to my cell mate, R. L. Conder, Jr., "I am not afraid to go. I have no more fear than walking out into the bright sunshine." This journal that I confide in, I will hold to my heart when I go. It will not survive anymore than I will.

"My attorney visited. Events in court went badly to-

day. Trial is set for September 15. I will not be judged by a jury of my peers. I will not sit and listen to Verona. I will not be humiliated by the stares of people who do not understand.

"Time is getting shorter now. I only have to live until August 30, and the suicide clause in my insurance policy will be moot, and my children will collect my life insurance. When I reflect, it seems the decent thing to do."

Dramatic scenario of the A. D. Payne case written by Megan Clark

8

"Well, the place looks lived in"
"Yeah, but by what?"

RICHARD ERDMAN
(Delong) and Dick Powell
(ex-con Rocky Malloy), CRY DANGER, 1951

Bruce Gorman's two-story limestone and brick mansion was enormous, with twelve-foot ceilings, windows as large as the ordinary door, polished stone floors, heavy velvet drapes, overstuffed furniture, a dining table that would seat twenty-four with room for all the necessary silver for a twelve-course meal. I didn't recognize some of the pieces of silver, but figured I would follow the rule of thumb and work from the outside in. My family were pioneer ranchers, so-called upper crust, but the ranch house I grew up in qualified for urban renewal compared to the Gorman mansion. Did I mention that the heap of stone and brick and porticos and Doric columns was incapable of being heated above sixty-five degrees? My strongest memory of the Gorman case, other than the sheer horror of it, was of being cold every time I stepped inside the front door. Perhaps the twisted evil we uncovered accounted for the cold, or perhaps it was the ghosts who walked the halls. Aren't ghosts associated with cold spots? There wasn't a spot in that house that wasn't cold. I couldn't imagine anyone actually living there, but especially Bruce Gorman, who seemed a warm and sympathetic man. After my first visit to that mausoleum, he had my sympathy.

The three of us were ushered into an entry hall larger than my living room by an honest-to-God butler. At least, I thought he was a butler, since I couldn't imagine anyone wearing a royal purple tailored jacket and white pleated shirt who wasn't paid to. After saying that he "would inform Mr. Gorman that we had arrived," he left us huddled together for warmth, Herb in his usual three piece, I in a heavy tweed jacket I almost hadn't worn because I thought it might make me sweat like a big dog, and Megan looking professional in a wool skirt and blazer. What profession I couldn't imagine, since not being a mystery reader, I don't have a good grasp of what constitutes haute couture for the female PI, but compared to Kinsey Millhone, Megan was overdressed. Good thing, too. In a T-shirt and jeans, she would have fallen victim to hypothermia within ten minutes. As it was, being smaller than average with a corresponding lesser body mass, Megan was more susceptible to the cold than Herb or I, so I guided her over to the fireplace, where a cheery blaze attempted and failed to warm the stone floors of the entry hall.

Megan held out her hands to warm them before the fire's heat vanished toward the two-story ceiling. "I toured several highland castles during a Scottish winter and wasn't this cold. Of course, the Scots hung wool tapestries on all the walls and brought thick Persian rugs back from the Crusades. Cut down on the drafts. It's only September. Imagine this place in January."

I shivered. "Enough to give you chilblains." I never was sure exactly what chilblains were, but every nineteenth-century novel I ever read mentioned them, so

I figured I was safe using the term in connection with the Gorman castle.

"Frostbite," said Megan. "Chilblains require moist cold, and there's no such thing in the Panhandle."

She was right about that. In a wet year, the Texas Panhandle receives somewhere on either side of eighteen inches of moisture from both rain and however many blizzards might blow in accompanied by a thirty-five- to forty-mile-an-hour wind. The most severe blizzards, affectionately known as 'blue northers,' come with fifty-plus-mile-an-hour winds. Have you ever seen it snowing horizontally? I have. Any man or animal outside without protection in a blue norther will die from hypothermia within minutes and freeze solid within hours. I could imagine this pile of aristocratic Gorman rock in a blue norther. You probably couldn't get warm if you set yourself on fire.

The faint rattle of doors sliding smoothly along oiled tracks on the wall opposite the fireplace announced the arrival of our host. Behind him I saw a large room with twelve-foot ceiling, comfortable-looking couches, wing chairs with matching ottomans, a marble fireplace large enough to roast a steer, several extraordinary oil paintings of Panhandle scenes—the lighthouse in Palo Duro Canyon being one—and numerous Tiffany lamps shedding pools of cozy golden light to fend off the darkness. What really attracted me to the room was the thick Persian rug that covered most of the floor. With an inch or two of closely woven wool between my feet and the stone floor, my toes might thaw by dinnertime.

"Megan Clark, Herb, Ryan, delighted to see you," said Bruce Gorman with a broad smile and an expression of relief in his eyes. "I don't know why Juan left you out here instead of escorting you into the parlor. I only leave politicians and bankers waiting in the entry hall. I've found that fifteen minutes out here, especially in the late fall and winter, makes either profession amenable to my proposals."

He offered his arm to Megan and escorted her through the open doors—which were approximately the size of the gate in *Jurassic Park*—with Herb and me following two steps behind like proper serfs, because serfs we were. I didn't believe for a minute that Juan of the royal purple jacket left us in that refrigerated meat locker on his own initiative. Like bankers and politicians, Mr. Bruce Gorman wanted us amenable. I wondered why.

Bruce Gorman stopped just inside the double doors and motioned Herb and me closer. "They've come, Miss Megan, gentlemen, all but Melinda's mom and brother. Neither one has spoken to the family in twenty years, so I guess I was overly optimistic in guaranteeing their attendance. But everyone else is here. They didn't have a choice. I still hold the purse strings in this family, and I'm not above writing anyone out of my will who fights me on this. The pen is indeed mightier than the sword, particularly if the pen is used to sign a will."

He stepped away, leaving the three of us together as an investigative conglomerate. "This is the lady and gentlemen I mentioned who will be asking you questions." Gorman's voice was a little louder than a conversational tone, but not by much. It didn't need to be. No one but him was talking.

He ushered us around the room, making introductions. I tried reading expressions on faces, but other than the sullen resentment evidenced by Jimmy Gorman, the suicide's younger brother, I might as well have tried reading the mansion's stone walls. *Guarded* is a good word to describe faces and eyes. Whoever said that eyes are windows to the soul never met the Gormans. Judging by their eyes, they didn't have souls.

Herb cleared his throat, something he always does before speaking. I guess you might call it a mannerism, and like most mannerisms, it becomes irritating over time. "Excuse me, Megan, but shouldn't we be questioning everyone in another room? So they won't hear what one another has to say?"

Megan stepped closer to Herb and lowered her voice to a whisper. "But I want them to hear one another. I'm sure they all have rehearsed their statements, since Bruce Gorman told them why he wanted them here tonight. What I'm interested in is what they each say to questions they never imagined I'd ask. Someone will slip up, and the rest will hear the slip and begin to think a little more deeply about that night. They will realize that one among their number is lying, and eventually someone will tell me who. As any cop can tell you, there is no such thing as honor among thieves, especially among thieves facing being written out of a will worth tens of millions of dollars. Somebody will roll over."

I was concerned—no, make that seriously concerned—about Megan's increased use of police vernacular and her shaky hold on reality. She was taking this whole amateur sleuth business to another level. She saw herself as that Kansas City reporter Gene Howe called in to solve the A. D. Payne case, but damn it all, this was the twenty-first century; amateur sleuths were out of style except in mystery novels.

Megan sat down on the couch across from Trent Gorman and his wife, Deanne, a tanned couple, groomed to the point of spit and polish and dressed in casual clothes sporting the latest designer signature in case you couldn't judge how expensive they were just by looking.

They were seated in wing chairs like royalty. But it was Megan who had the attendants, even though Herb and I didn't wear silk stockings and knee pants, and lounged on either side of our redheaded princess instead of standing at attention.

"You're Randy's older brother?" she asked, at ease and focused on his answer. It took more than clothes to either impress or intimidate Megan Clark.

By my reckoning, Trent Gorman was a man in his early forties—in other words, my age—but he was fighting age to a standstill. I supposed his dark brown hair might be natural, but I doubted it. Few men our age are without at least a sprinkling of gray hair. And we all have a few lines on our faces, particularly around the eyes. Trent's face was as smooth as a baby's bottom. I never had much use for cosmetic surgery. It always seemed either another way to deny reality or a mask to hide behind. Megan always referred to subjects of obvious face-lifts as suffering from the Dorian Gray syndrome. She was of the age and generation to be merciless in her criticism.

"Yes, I am," replied Trent. Then words burst loose that he had obviously rehearsed. It sounded more like lines in film noir than normal conversation. "I don't know what you hope to find out after all this time, Miss Clark, other than that my brother committed suicide. He murdered himself, and that's the only person he murdered. He was murderer and victim all in one. That's all I know other than I wish my grandfather had left it alone."

"Actually, Trent—you don't mind if I call you Trent, do you? With everyone's last name being Gorman, it seems the logical way to distinguish one Gorman from another without the awkwardness of saying Mr. Trent

Gorman or Mr. Paul Gorman, etc. Don't you agree?"

What choice did he have except to be a churlish snob? He agreed.

"Actually, Trent, I'm not here to investigate Randy's suicide. I'm here to find Melinda Gorman's murderer."

I don't know if Megan deliberately raised her voice or if it was an unconscious act on her part, but she stopped all conversation better than a gag. That room was quiet enough to hear the proverbial pin drop. All eyes focused on the slight figure in the black blazer and skirt, and not a single one was friendly except her two brothers in crime: Herb and me. Even Bruce Gorman looked taken aback by Megan's announcement, but I don't know what else he expected. If you hire Megan Clark to investigate a murder, you've bought yourself a loose cannon.

Deanne Gorman, Trent's blonde-by-request wife, was the first to recover. Her face, too, was smooth as a baby's bottom but with the texture of fine cowhide and about the same color. Despite her lack of wrinkles, compared to Megan she looked like a sun-damaged old hag. If she wasn't already making quarterly trips to the dermatologist for treatment of skin cancer, she would be soon.

Deanne rose and leaned over Megan, and I caught the acrid scent of a chemical-based perfume. I prefer the natural scents myself: roses or lilacs. "Let the dead bury the dead, Miss Clark. I don't care who murdered Melinda. Pointing the finger at someone now won't bring back Randy. It's just such a shame that he married that blue-collar secretary in the first place. You shouldn't mix with the help. If he hadn't, he might still be alive." With that statement, she whirled around and sat back down in her wing chair with the aplomb of the queen in *Snow White*.

To someone who uses socioeconomic class as an adjective, not a judgment, and to someone who furthermore was solidly middle class and proud of it, Deanne's words called for a frontal assault. Megan rose, and I felt her bristle like a little redheaded porcupine—or a Celt with a dab of Cherokee whose honor has been impinged, which is infinitely worse. I hastily scooted to one end of the couch to clear the field of battle. I wasn't leaving Megan to fend for herself; I was getting out of her way.

"You're saying it's all right to murder the help?" asked Megan in that sweet voice that concealed the sting in her words until it was too late.

Deanne looked blank for a moment as if she didn't understand the question, and she probably didn't. That's what comes of only associating with those of like mind and social class. You aren't used to having your opinions challenged. "I didn't say that. Don't put words in my mouth!"

"I don't need to," said Megan. "You called her 'the help' and inferred that if she had stayed in her place, Randy Gorman would still be alive. She was your sister-in-law, whether you liked her or not, and her murder led directly to Randy's suicide, so you should care who murdered her. But you don't, so I can only assume that it's all right to kill the help."

Deanne turned a particularly unattractive shade of fuchsia, I assume because rawhide and blushes don't blend well together. "That's not what I meant!" she exclaimed, looking at her husband for help.

But Trent Gorman was too busy studying Megan as if she was an alien species he found interesting. Or perhaps he had noted his wife's dilemma but chose to let

Deanne extract herself from her own verbal faux pas.

Megan sat down on the ottoman in front of Deanne's chair, smoothed her skirt over her knees, crossed her ankles, and slanted her legs to the left in the perfect sorority-girl pose. Not that she was a sorority girl, but she executed the poses perfectly when necessary. It helped that she wasn't wearing her usual cut-offs, T-shirt, and hiking boots.

"Then tell me what you did mean," said Megan. "I don't want to misunderstand you on such an important issue."

"I merely meant," began Deanne, then fell silent with her mouth open as she struggled to find the right words. "Of course I was horrified that Melinda was murdered, but if Randy hadn't married her, then she would be alive and so would he."

"Then you believe that she was murdered because she married Randy Gorman?"

Deanne stared at Megan, her expression blank as she struggled to find an answer. Finally, she shook her head and looked down at the floor. "I don't know."

"Where were you that night?"

"In the library—on the other side of the hall—reading a book. The library is the warmest room in the house—if you wrap up in an afghan." When I heard that, I was all in favor of moving to the library and passing out afghans.

"What were you reading?"

Deanne looked startled for a moment. "A novel I took from the library. I don't remember the exact title right now, but it was something like *The Winthrop Woman*. What I read was interesting, but I never finished it."

"Why not?"

"Randy discovered Melinda's body, and I can't think

of that book without remembering the rest of the evening, and I never wanted to pick it up again."

"Did the main character remind you of Melinda?"

Deanne suddenly looked as old as her real age. "I guess a little bit she did."

Megan turned to Trent. "Do you agree with your wife, Trent? Was Melinda murdered because she married your brother?"

"I don't know how you can come to that conclusion from my wife's answers."

Megan smiled and tilted her head to look at him. If Trent Gorman thought the fact that he was now standing and she was sitting would work to his psychological advantage, he didn't know Megan or her psychology.

"Elementary linguistic decoding skills."

As a conversation stopper, Megan's answer was worth at least an eight. However, to stop Trent Gorman's superciliousness, a blunt instrument was required.

"I'm multilingual in Latin, ancient Greek, Hebrew, Arabic, Old English as well as the modern variety, and Old French. Decoding your wife's answers wasn't difficult." Left unsaid were the words *you doofus*.

Trent apparently got the message because he turned red—or fuchsia, given that he was the same rawhide color as his wife. "I think Deanne meant that there is no point in digging up the past. My brother is dead, and so is his wife."

"Then you don't believe that Melinda was killed because she married your brother?"

"Believe me, *Doctor* Clark, despite my wife's clumsy way with words, we don't murder the help."

"But she wasn't the help anymore, was she, Trent? She was family."

"We tried to accept her as family, yes."

"Did you succeed?"

"Did we what?" asked Trent, like his wife, looking as if he didn't understand the question. I don't imagine many people are in a position to question Trent Gorman about anything, much less something so sensitive as relationships when the help become family.

"Succeed?" asked Megan. "You said you tried to accept her as family, and I asked if you succeeded."

"We didn't have a chance to succeed or fail. She was murdered the night they came back from a three-week honeymoon. Three weeks is not enough time to adjust."

"It was long enough for someone to build up a ferocious hatred."

"I don't know about that. I only know that I didn't kill my brother's wife."

"Melinda."

"What?" Again Trent looked confused. Judging by his answers, he either had something to hide or he wasn't very good at decoding Megan's questions. I would bet on the former.

"Your brother's wife. Her name was Melinda."

"Yes, I knew that. She was a secretary at Gorman Oil."

"Where were you when she was murdered?"

I saw a muscle clench in his jaw before he answered. "I was playing bridge with my grandfather, my mother, and Melinda's mother, Janice Mitchell."

"Did anyone leave the room while he or she was dummy?"

"I don't remember. Twenty years is a long time."

"Yes, it is. It's long enough for Randy and Melinda to have raised a family—if someone hadn't murdered them."

"What are you talking about?" demanded Trent Gorman. "Randy wasn't murdered. He killed himself."

"To use your wife's logic, if Melinda hadn't been murdered, he wouldn't have committed suicide. Thus, whoever murdered Melinda also murdered Randy."

Sometimes Megan's logic leaves me gaping like a goldfish, too.

9

"You're trying to make me go soft. Well, you can save your oil. I don't go soft for anybody."

ALAN LADD
(hired killer Philip Raven) to Veronica Lake
(undercover agent Ellen Graham),
This Gun for Hire, 1942

"I don't know why my father insists on our talking to you. There is nothing to say. Randy is dead, Melinda is dead, and they are the only ones who know the answers."

Paul Gorman had to be in his sixties, but he didn't look it. Neither did he look to have had a face lift. The lines around the eyes, the grooves from the nose to the mouth were there, but his throat and chin were still more firm than not. Whereas his son, Trent, looked artificially enhanced, Paul Gorman looked natural, and Megan thought that he was. He was aging gracefully in the way some men did, Ryan for instance, so that he actually was more handsome in his forties, fifties, and sixties than he was in his twenties or thirties. From a strictly physical viewpoint, Megan bet more women would hit on Paul Gorman than Trent.

That didn't mean that he was more truthful.

"I assume you mean that Melinda knew her murderer,

and Randy had an overpowering reason for committing suicide."

Paul's eyes were the color of a London fog and concealed as much. "I don't believe that's what I said."

"But that's what I heard," said Megan, getting a little tired of the Gormans' verbal gymnastics. Given the number of split hairs floating in the air, she would have thought she was at a lawyers' convention. "Maybe you could clear up your meaning."

"The answers to your questions have been buried in the cemetery for twenty years. I have no answers for you."

"Then how about guesses. Who do you suspect of killing Melinda?"

"I don't care to speculate, since I don't know what men she had been involved with before she married my son."

"But you believe a man killed her?"

"She was strangled. Doesn't that mean a man, and a man with a very personal motive? I told the police repeatedly to look for a lover, but they ignored me."

Megan wondered if Paul Gorman really thought her stupid. "Assuming she had a lover, he must have had access to the pool cues in this house, since the police proved she was struck down with a pool cue before she was strangled. Would you care to speculate further in light of that fact?"

Paul Gorman was silent for a moment, an expression of chilly dislike in his gray eyes. "Do you want me to say that my son killed his wife?"

"Only if it's what you believe."

"I believe nothing, Dr. Clark, except that you are trampling on the feelings of this family, and I will not provide you with any opinions that you may twist into new questions."

"Where were you at the time of the murder?" asked Megan. "Surely that's not an opinion I can bend out of shape."

"I was playing pool with my son, my nephew Jake Gorman, and Tommy Mitchell, Melinda's brother."

"How many times did you leave the room?"

"Once that I recall. I went to the kitchen to see about more beer and snacks."

"So you returned with beer and pretzels."

"I didn't return with anything. I spoke with the butler about refreshments."

"So you spoke to Juan—"

"Juan was not employed by my father at that time. Earl Washington was the butler, and he's dead now, so I'm afraid I'm without an alibi except that I'm sure everyone remembers the shrimp butter sandwiches that night."

"Did anyone else leave the room?"

"Obviously my son did, but I don't remember anyone else. It's been twenty years, and the subsequent events of the evening wiped out everything that had gone on before."

"So Randy went to look for his wife?"

"Yes, he did."

"Where did he look?"

Paul Gorman looked exasperated. "I suppose he looked upstairs in their bedroom before he went to the gazebo."

"Why did he go to the gazebo?"

"I don't know, Dr. Clark. It didn't seem to matter why, once he was there."

"Did he carry a pool cue with him when he went upstairs?"

"I don't know. I didn't notice. Now, I've told you everything I did, everything I know."

"Not quite, Paul. Do you believe that your son killed his wife?"

"I don't believe it matters anymore what I think or any member of this family thinks. The fact is that Randy is dead."

"I think it matters very much what you think, because if Randy didn't murder his wife, then someone else did."

Megan didn't add the words *in this room,* but she thought Paul Gorman got the point because his lips tightened, deepening the grooves around his mouth. Given the silence among the rest of the Gormans, they got the point, too, which is what she intended. Divide and conquer was sound strategy. Before long, the Gormans would be ratting out each other to avoid becoming suspects.

She hoped.

Of course, a family who had presented a united front for twenty years was a formidable opponent. But someone would give away the farm. She would bet on it.

Megan turned to Paul's wife and Randy Gorman's mother, Michele, a tall woman as stately in her own way as her husband, but gray hair and lines and grooves and sagging skin under her chin and on her throat made her look every year of her age, if not more. If a son's suicide had only lightly touched Paul Gorman physically, it had blighted whatever youth had remained to his wife.

"I have one son dead, *Miss* Clark. Do you expect me to point the finger at another of my sons? I don't care who killed Melinda. I just want my family left alone."

Megan nearly flinched at the venom in her voice, particularly when she said *Miss* Clark.

"You think because I am single and childless that I don't understand how you feel," said Megan, sensing that she was treading through a minefield of emotions. One wrong step, and this woman could fly to pieces.

"Until you have carried a child, delivered him in pain, cherished him, only to see him take his life over some slut, you can't possibly know what I feel."

"Do you know for a fact that Melinda was a slut?" asked Megan, thinking that if she had any sense at all, she would take Ryan's advice, forget the Gormans, write a paper for some popular history magazine on the Boyce-Sneed feud, and return to her quiet life as an assistant reference librarian. Come to think of it, she wasn't even being paid to delve into the psyche of this dysfunctional family.

"I saw her at Gorman Oil Company every time I stopped by. She was leaning over the men, pointing out something in a letter or some report, pushing her breasts against the back of their shoulders, or standing close to them, playing with the buttons on their shirts. And laughing at everything they said, throwing her head back and whinnying like some horse. And wearing clothes that were too low, too short, and too tight. She was cheap, and she brought her cheapness along with her when she married into this family. Oh, I tried to tell Randy about her, but he would get so furious and slam out of the room. He finally moved in with his grandfather just to get away from me, and it hurts me to this day that I chased him out of his home with my nagging." She stopped and dabbed her eyes with a handkerchief.

Paul Gorman sat on the arm of her chair and put his arm around his wife's shoulders. "I think we've had enough of your questions, Dr. Clark. My wife has never recovered from the death of our son, and your meddling is aggravating her condition."

Megan decided she had never seen such cold eyes in her life as the ones Paul Gorman turned on her. Glacierlike was the closest description she could think of. But she had been glared at by experts. Until you've crossed an archaeology professor by picking up an artifact without photographing it first, you have no idea what fury really is.

"Which men did Melinda flirt with?"

"I *said* that's enough!" said Paul Gorman through clenched teeth.

"Everyone!" Michele burst out. "No one was safe from her! No one!"

"Michele!" said Paul in a stern voice. "Be quiet now. Don't think about it anymore. It's past. It happened twenty years ago."

"Megan," said Herb in a hesitant voice. "I think it would be wise to stop now. Mrs. Gorman appears to be very upset."

"Paul, do you think Melinda was killed because she married your son?"

"Leave my family alone!" cried Michele Gorman, twisting her handkerchief in her hands.

Megan sighed. "I'm sorry that I've upset you, Michele, but I will get at the truth."

Michele Gorman gave her a terrified look. "Leave us alone, please."

Megan felt Ryan grasp her arm. "Give it a rest, Megan, before Mrs. Gorman has hysterics, and Bruce Gorman calls Juan to give us the bum's rush out the front door. My ego can't stand being thrown out by somebody who wears a purple jacket."

10

"I may have romanticized you before, but now I know you. You're something from under a rock."

MARSHA HUNT
(Ann Martin) to Dennis O'Keefe (Her boyfriend,
gangster Joe Sullivan),
Raw Deal, 1948

I had a death grip on Megan's arm, and I didn't intend to let go until she was on the other side of the room from the unstable Mrs. Paul Gorman. "Come on, Megan," I said, my voice as soft as it would go without turning into a whisper. "It's very uncouth to cause a nervous breakdown in one of the dinner guests. It will get you blackballed from society parties."

"Society doesn't know who I am anyway—and let go of my arm. You're leaving a bruise." Her voice was low, but there wasn't anything soft about it.

"I'm not squeezing hard enough to leave a bruise. You just want me to let go so you can go back to Paul and Michele Gorman and ask another question."

Herb was trotting—since Herb is the sort to trot—on the other side of Megan, dabbing at his forehead with a pristine white handkerchief. Everything about Herb is pristine. I was surprised his sweat glands even functioned. "Ryan is right, Megan. Michele Gorman was building toward an emotional eruption," he whispered.

Then his eyes widened as if he had just recognized a universal truth. "I like that phrase, don't you? Emotional eruption? I think I'll use it in my book."

"You do that, Herb," I said. "It's a pithy phrase, spice up your narrative." I hoped God wasn't listening, because if he was, I was scheduled to be struck by lightning for lying. Herb's book needed more than a pithy phrase to save it. His book was so deadly boring, it needed resuscitating.

Megan twisted her arm out of my grip. "I don't need to be led away like a kid pestering the grown-ups. Besides, I didn't have any more questions at the moment for Michele or Paul Gorman. I learned what I needed to know for the present."

Herb looked puzzled, and I'm sure I did, too. "Exactly what did you learn? That Michele Gorman thought Melinda was a slut. It doesn't take a rocket scientist to figure out that the family would dump on Melinda and lie to cover up for each other," I said, looking at said Gormans, who were looking at us, ears perked to eavesdrop and appearing frustrated that we were speaking too quietly to be overheard.

"I don't mind the lies. Since I didn't expect anyone to confess this evening, then lies are fine, as long as everyone heard them—which everybody did. One of the people in this room will recognize the lie, and like acid, it will begin to eat away at his conscience, particularly when I point out to each one privately that if Randy didn't kill his wife, then some other family member did, and as Jerry Carr said, let Randy take the fall."

"You're assuming the Gormans have consciences like real people," I said, barely moving my lips in case any of the family could lip-read.

"If they don't, I'll point out that anyone who would

kill one family member would not be adverse to killing another if, in the murderer's estimation, it became necessary."

I always knew that Megan had a devious mind, and that bit of strategy proved it. For pure deviousness, the Gormans had met their match.

"Have you even considered that Randy might have really killed his wife and really did kill himself out of remorse?" I asked. "Isn't that at least a remote possibility?"

"It would make a nice plot twist in a mystery novel, but I don't believe it. I don't believe a man who defied his family, or at least, his mother, to marry the woman he loved, would kill her after a three-week honeymoon. They didn't even have time to have their first fight." Megan shook her head. "No, Randy didn't kill Melinda. That solution feels wrong."

"Excuse me, but I thought amateur sleuths worked with clues and evidence and such that the police had overlooked. What's this 'it feels wrong'? Women's intuition?"

That earned me a sharp look, and to tell the truth, I was sorry I brought it up. Megan has a theory that women's intuition is nothing more than the female's collecting and coding data, including emotional nuances, on the subconscious level. Her opinion is that because it is done on the subconscious level, and women are unable to precisely describe the process by which they reach a particular conclusion, men brush it aside as guesswork. Of course, Megan being Megan, she can track the various connections between data and conclusion as far as her own intuition goes, but then she's an anthropologist and used to dealing with how minds work. As for me, even after having been married for twenty-two years be-

fore I became a widower, I barely have a clue as to how
a woman's mind works on the conscious level; the subconscious is beyond my ken.

"I'll discuss it with you later, Ryan, when you're in
a more reasonable mood. For now, I want to talk to Jake
Gorman. And if you gentlemen don't mind, please don't
interrupt me this time."

She walked—actually, stalked is a better word—toward the fireplace where Jake Gorman relaxed on one
end of a couch upholstered in what looked like brocaded
gold satin. Jake had to be in his very late thirties or
maybe very early forties if my memory of the case
served. He was a handsome man, dark blond hair and
beard as opposed to his brunette cousins. With all the
facial hair, any lines and grooves and loose flesh under
the chin was camouflaged. What wasn't camouflaged
was the cold look in his blue eyes. Much colder, and his
irises would freeze.

Megan sat down on the couch a scarce two feet from
him. I thought it was a bravado sort of gesture, sitting
that close to someone who made no secret of despising
you.

She held out her hand, but Jake ignored her gesture.
Megan shrugged when it became obvious that Jake had
no intention of shaking hands with her. The only snub
that really hurt her was the snub by academia when she
applied for a teaching fellowship while working on her
master's at the University of Texas. Insulted, Megan
went to the University of Chicago instead.

"You're Jake Gorman?" she asked.

Instead of answering, Jake Gorman looked her up and
down as if he suspected she had some sort of social
disease. "Do you like playing in the mud, *Doctor* Clark?
Because that's what you're doing, and then you're dirt-

ying the Gorman family with your muddy hands. Melinda's dead, Randy's dead, leave them in whatever kind of peace they've found."

"I'll assume from your answer that you're Jake Gorman. Tell me, Jake, do you think Melinda was murdered because she married your cousin?"

"I don't know why she was murdered, but presumedly she angered the murderer so much that he strangled her."

Megan sat up straighter, and I saw her eyes narrow ever so slightly, both actions a danger signal to anyone who knew her. "You're saying it's Melinda's fault that she was murdered?"

"Not necessarily, but I believe strangulation is a very personal kind of murder, unlike a gunshot, which allows some distance between victim and murderer, so I have to assume someone wanted her dead very badly to wrap his hands around her throat and squeeze like a boa constrictor killing its prey." He shifted on the couch and put his arm on its back, a very relaxed and arrogant pose, pleased with himself for his simile.

"Except the boa constrictor only kills to survive, and Melinda was not prey; she was a bride who hoped to live happily with her new family," said Megan. I noticed her gradually turning red, a sure indicator of Herb's new phrase: an emotional eruption.

Jake Gorman shrugged his shoulders.

"Why do you suppose someone was so angry with Melinda that he killed her?"

"I wouldn't know."

"Were you one of the men Melinda flirted with while she was at Gorman Oil?"

"I don't fraternize with the employees."

"But Michele Gorman just said that Melinda flirted with everyone."

Jake Gorman turned the color of a brick. I've always thought a blushing blond was very unattractive. "I never said *she* didn't flirt with me; just that I didn't flirt with her."

"Fraternize."

"What?"

"You said you didn't *fraternize* with the help."

"Don't try to twist my words, *Doctor* Clark."

"I'll try very hard not to, but you're making it difficult," said Megan. "Let's return to a former question. Do you think Melinda was murdered because she married your cousin?"

"And I'll give my former answer: I have no idea."

"Would you care to speculate?"

"No, I would not care to speculate who killed Melinda with the pool cue in the gazebo."

Megan folded her hands, a sublimation of what she probably really wanted to do, which was punch Jake Gorman in the nose. Certainly I was close to doing it.

"Where were you during the time of the murder?" asked Megan.

"You already know. My uncle Paul told you. I was playing pool."

"Did you leave the room?"

"I don't remember. Probably to go to the bathroom."

"What did you do with your pool cue?"

"I don't know, probably put it back in the case. I certainly wouldn't have laid it down anywhere, not with Tommy Mitchell drinking and staggering around. I spent the whole evening waiting for him to stick his cue through the felt top of the pool table like he was one of the three stooges."

"Tommy Mitchell was inebriated?"

"No, *Doctor* Clark. Inebriated is too classy a term. He was drunk."

That did it. I was tired of the Gormans addressing Megan as though she were a medicine show quack instead of a Ph.D.

I leaned over Jake Gorman until I was almost literally in his face and grabbed his tie. "You'll address Megan with respect, or I'll haul you through those French doors over there to the backyard and kick your snobbish backside to kingdom come."

I felt Herb pulling at my arm. "Please excuse Professor Stevens's rhetoric, Mr. Gorman. He is very protective of Dr. Clark. Ryan, let go of Mr. Gorman's tie. I believe he is having trouble breathing.

"Ryan," said Megan. "Remember, you don't want to be thrown out by a man who wears a purple coat."

I let go of Jake Gorman's tie and watched him loosen it until the purple color receded from his face and he seemed to be breathing easier. "Remember what I said, Gorman, and we'll get along fine."

I straightened up, gave everyone a Clint-Eastwood-as-Dirty-Harry-after-he's-blown-away-the-bad-guys smile, and rested against one end of the fireplace, which was the warmest place I'd been all night.

"You assaulted me!" accused Jake Gorman, his color mostly back to normal and his eyes back in their sockets. "My attorney will be calling you."

"I don't think so, Jake," said Bruce Gorman, the first time he'd spoken since he introduced us. "You were disrespectful, and Professor Stevens took you to task for it. If he had not, I would have deducted a generous amount from your paycheck at Gorman Oil as a reminder that I don't allow my guests to be insulted. Money seems to be the language best understood by this family. My apologies, Dr. Clark, for the ill manners of my family. It won't happen again."

His white eyebrows were drawn together in a frown as he glanced at each member of his family. My question was: Why did he wait until I had taken care of the matter to warn his family against rudeness? Everyone had been rude and obstreperous. Why wait until I had nearly strangled his jerk of a grandson before he said something? I'm not an amateur sleuth—I merely record the adventures of one—but it appeared to me that everyone in the room had a different agenda, including Bruce Gorman.

Megan tilted her head in acknowledgment of Bruce Gorman's apology, but I saw her white knuckles as she clasped her hands in her lap. She was running on grit alone, and her tank was nearly empty.

"So Tommy Mitchell was drunk. Did he leave the room at any time?"

"Naturally, to use the facilities. You know how it is when you drink."

Megan shook her head. "Actually, I don't know, since I don't drink much myself, but I'll take your word for it as you seem to have some knowledge of the subject." The jab was subtle, but she drew blood, judging by the sudden flare of Jake Gorman's nostrils.

She smiled at Jake and continued. "Did you see your cousin, Randy Gorman, leave the room?"

Jake Gorman looked at Megan with a triumphant expression. "Yes, I did, twice. Once with a pool cue and once without it."

It was a blow, and I saw Megan blink as she absorbed the force of it. "Did you see Randy come back into the room carrying his pool cue?"

Jake Gorman studied his fingernails—nicely manicured, I noticed. Why is it I've never trusted a man with a manicure?

"I didn't notice, *Doctor* Clark." This time he smiled at her and settled comfortably back in the corner of the couch and folded his arms as if a debate was over, and he had won.

"I'm not the only one with muddy hands, Jake Gorman. You just did a handy job defacing your cousin's tomb. If I reveal that Randy was innocent of murdering his wife, will you have the decency to feel ashamed?"

Megan rose and walked across the room toward the last of the Gormans to be the subject of her interrogation.

11

Jimmy Gorman looked wasted to Megan. Not wasted as in drug abuse, but in the sense that life had stopped for him before he had quite grown up. He wore Levi's and a T-shirt under a blazer and no socks with his dock shoes, an all right outfit for an eighties TV star, but out of sync for the beginning of the twenty-first century. Unlike his father and brother, his hair was a light brown and his face covered with out of fashion stubble. There was an unhealthy softness to his face and chin, as if he hadn't outgrown his baby fat. Physically he was a thirty-six-year-old man caught in transition from teenager to adult, unable to retreat into his past but equally unable to advance into the present. The future, Megan thought, would be forever beyond his reach.

"Jimmy Gorman?" Megan asked, as if he could be anyone else.

He lounged in one of a pair of white brocade wing chairs in the corner adjacent to a pair of bifold doors to what Megan later learned with the formal dining room. On the other wall was a pair of French doors leading to the side portico. With both his legs hanging over one arm of the chair as if he was sixteen again, he looked like an awkward, aging youth, but he stumbled up when Megan spoke to him, unlike Jake Gorman who never stood up to acknowledge Megan's presence. Ordinarily, Megan didn't think too much about the old-fashioned manners of a gentleman, but she found herself judging the Gorman men by the presence or lack of such manners. It was the house, she thought. In a castle, one expects chivalrous behavior.

"Yeah, I'm Jimmy Gorman. Pleased to meet ya," he said, holding out his hand.

Surprised, Megan shook his hand and found it hard and callused. "Please sit down, I'll sit across from you in this other chair."

"So you're the woman Grandpa hired to exorcize the ghosts." His husky voice was low, as if he didn't want anyone but Megan to hear him.

"Your grandfather hired me to find out who murdered Melinda Gorman." Megan lowered her own voice to match his.

"Same difference. You couldn't pay me to go out to that gazebo at night, and I won't sleep in Randy's old room, either. Say, do you believe in channeling?"

Megan shook her head. "I don't believe in ghosts, and I don't believe in channeling, either. I'm a scientist, well, actually an anthropologist, but anywhere else in the world except the United States, that makes me a scientist. So you believe that Randy's and Melinda's ghosts haunt this house?"

"Just Randy's. Melinda stays in the gazebo and backyard. Grandpa's old cook saw her once a week or so after the murder, still wearing that long white and robe, her blonde hair falling down her back. But Randy walks the upstairs hall, just like he did before he shot himself. I was here that day, and he just kept walking up and down the hall with a wall-eyed look."

"What do you mean by a wall-eyed look, Jimmy?" asked Megan, wondering if there was a single Gorman who was stable—and normal. Actually, Jimmy was stable; it was just that his stability ran to being nuts.

Jimmy made a meaningless gesture with one hand. "You know, kind of wild, like a cow that lost her calf or a coyote that's caught in a trap—desperate like. I work out at the ranch mostly," he said, "so I'm always making comparisons like that. If you want a better definition than that, I can't give you one."

"So your cousin looked desperate that last day. Did anything happen that might have made him desperate? Did the police question him again that day? Was it an anniversary of the first time he met Melinda, or of when he proposed?" asked Megan, wishing she had asked the other Gormans if they had seen or talked to Randy that day. She needed collaboration of Jimmy's statements.

"The police hadn't talked to him that I know of. You'll have to ask Dad or Grandad about that. They were both here that day. And I don't think it was the anniversary of anything, and I'd probably know, because he talked to me more than anybody about him and Melinda. And it was still a week or so shy of the anniversary of her murder, so I don't think that set him off."

"Did you talk to him at all that day? Did he give you any hint of what he was about to do?"

"Don't you think I would have done something to stop him if I had known he was about to swallow his forty-five? I asked him kind of casual what was wrong, and he just stared at me. I told him that his pacing up and down the halls was driving me nuts. You know what he said? He said, "Jimmy, everything's gone that I believed in." What do you think he meant by that, Doctor Clark? Because I sure couldn't tell you. I figured he meant God, but I don't think that was what he was talking about, and I didn't have sense enough to ask. I was a stupid dumb kid all tied up in my own problems."

He sat looking across the room through the limestone walls as though he saw something no one else could see. "You know, I was only sixteen, and all I had my mind on was sex, cars, and beer. I was shocked when Melinda was murdered, but I wasn't shocked when Randy committed suicide. You know what I was instead? I was just damn mad. I was already a social outcast because of the murder and Randy's being suspected; the suicide was just the icing on the cake. You ought to be the object of a whispering campaign, Dr. Clark. I couldn't buy a date, and when I did, all she wanted to do was see the gazebo and talk about how it felt to be the brother of a murderer. It took me a long time to switch from being angry Randy committed suicide to hurting over it. But it's like that gunshot took my life, too, except I'm still walking around, and Randy's under the ground out at Llano Cemetery."

He swiped his eyes on his blazer to blot the tears Megan had seen in the soft lamplight. "I don't mean to sound like a whiner, Dr. Clark. I'm better when I'm out at the ranch working with the cattle and the horses. That's dirty, hard work that's clean, if you know what I mean. I'm busy out there, and I don't think so much."

Megan nodded her head because she didn't trust herself to speak. Too many tears clogged her throat.

"I'm ashamed of being so mad about Randy's suicide. I was a selfish little bastard, just thinking of myself."

Megan leaned toward him, wondering if he had never

discussed his feelings with his family, and if not, why not. Why had he kept such feelings inside for twenty years? "Jimmy, you were sixteen years old. I don't think there's a sixteen-year-old alive who isn't sure that life revolves around him like the earth revolves around the sun. Youth is self-centered and selfish. Your anger was absolutely normal. Besides, I can't believe that you didn't feel some grief along with that anger. Didn't you feel a little bit blue?"

Jimmy looked at her as if she had tossed him a life jacket just as the *Titanic* was going down, and Megan felt uncomfortable. She didn't have much practice doing grief counseling, and besides, she had to be objective. Jimmy might have murdered Melinda and all of his guilt and shame was because his act triggered the suicide. There was a reason why Jimmy Gorman believed his brother's ghost walked the halls, and she needed to find it.

"Where were you on the night of the murder, Jimmy?"

"I ate dinner and left on a date. Grandad let me take his new Continental. Man, but I though I was slick. I picked up this girl I was dating, Amy Phillips was her name, and we took off for Western Plaza to go to the show. The police came in and hauled us both out of the theater. Talk about embarrassing. Amy huddled in the front seat and bawled and never dated me again. The police followed me the whole way to Amy's house and then back to Grandad's. They just told me Melinda was dead, and I was needed at home. I didn't know it was murder until I got back here."

"Tell me about dinner that night, Jimmy. Was it a happy occasion?" asked Megan, wondering why she got more emotional nuances about Randy, Melinda, and the murder from Jimmy Gorman, who by his own admission was oblivious to much besides sex, cars, and beer, than she did from the rest of the Gormans put together. Except one Gorman. One Gorman had inadvertently revealed a treasure trove of emotional nuances, if she could only figure out what it all meant.

"Randy was flying high, he was so happy, but Melinda was more like she was determined than happy. She was pretty, all that blonde hair and a bright yellow dress. She looked like a jonquil, and jonquils have always been my favorite flower, I guess because they're one of the first up in the spring, like . . . like an omen for good things to come. But that yellow dress didn't bring her luck, did it?"

Megan folded her hands to keep from reaching over and patting Jimmy on the head. "Why do you say Melinda seemed determined? Determined about what?"

Jimmy gestured at the room. "To fit in with all this."

Megan looked around the huge room, noticing that all the rest of the Gormans were focused on her and Jimmy. She tried to imagine herself in Melinda's place, tried to imagine changing herself into a faux Michele or faux Deanne, and failed. Megan knew there was no way she would surrender her own personality to win anybody's approval, but she thought she knew why Melinda would try so hard. Melinda Gorman married above herself, as the expression goes, and she wanted her marriage to succeed so badly that she would sacrifice her own identity, if that's what it took. Megan suspected that hell would have frozen over before Melinda won either Deanne's or Michele's approval. Except to her husband and Jimmy, and maybe Bruce Gorman, Melinda would forever be "the help."

"Jimmy, do you believe that Melinda was killed because she married your brother?"

"I heard you ask Jake that question, and I've been thinking about it. I can't see any other reason for somebody to murder her, whether it was Randy or some old boyfriend. Somebody was jealous."

"Do you believe that Randy killed Melinda?"

Jimmy leaned over, resting his elbows on his thighs, and put his hands over his face. "I gotta believe he did," he said in a muffled, low voice, impossible to hear beyond a few feet.

Megan averted her head. She didn't think she could watch the grieving boy-man in the opposite chair. She wondered to what she had committed herself and Murder by the Yard. All she had found at the Gorman mansion was a wasted life, a blighted family, a patriarch seeking help to drain a wound of poison.

Ryan abruptly seized Megan's hand and hauled her to her feet. He slid his arm around her waist and leaned down to whisper, so only she and Herb could hear. Certainly the rest of the Gormans couldn't. As for Jimmy, Megan doubted he was even conscious of where he was.

"Let's make our excuses and go home and thaw out. I don't think I can sit in that dining room and pretend all is well. And I don't want you subjected to any more poison that passes for conversation among the Gormans," said Ryan.

"You can't blame them for being nasty. I was asking very personal questions," said Megan.

"Which Grandpa Gorman asked them to answer. I wasn't very impressed with their obedience. I don't think anybody but Jimmy and Grandpa gives a damn what happened twenty years ago, and they resent your asking questions. Come on, Megan, give it up for tonight. Let the Gormans dine alone in dysfunctional luxury," said Ryan.

Herb shivered as he looked around the cavernous room. "This would make a fine set for *The Haunting of Hill House*."

Megan leaned against Ryan. He was strong and solid and sensible, while everyone else in the room was unstable and slightly nuts. "There are even two ghosts."

"So tell the Gormans to hire an exorcist," said Ryan. "You don't qualify because you don't wear a backward collar."

Megan stood by while Ryan excused them from dinner with the light touch of the upper crust getting out of something they didn't want to do without insulting the host. She had never really thought of Ryan as a member of one of the founding families of the Panhandle until now. He had always been Ryan, her best friend's father and now her best friend. She wondered if best friends noticed one another's sex appeal, and if they didn't, what her suddenly noticing that Ryan was very handsome and distinguished and sexy might really mean. Especially the sexy part.

But the puzzle of Ryan's sexy good looks and their sudden effect on her abruptly disappeared from her thought processes when Paul Gorman caught up with them at the front door.

"Excuse me, Doctor Clark, if I might have a word with you," he asked.

"Certainly," said Megan, disengaging herself from Ryan's arm and straightening her blazer.

"This is very private."

"These gentlemen are my confidants. Anything you say to me will eventually be told to them, so they might as well hear it firsthand."

Paul looked displeased, and Megan found she didn't care. She didn't like his response to her searching out the truth about his son, and to be honest, she didn't much like him. In fact, she didn't much like any of the Gormans except Jimmy.

"I don't know what my son, Jimmy, told you, Doctor Clark, and I'm not asking you to tell me, but I feel that you ought to know that Jimmy had a nervous breakdown after Randy's suicide. He was institutionalized for six months and subjected to intense therapy. Before his breakdown, he showed a gift for the oil and gas business. We—my father and I—expected him to take his place in Gorman Oil Company and eventually run the operation after I retired. Then came his breakdown, and afterward—well, about all he can cope with is working on the family ranch. He is competent at running our cattle operation, sometimes even shows a flair at marketing, but he is nothing like he was before the breakdown. He told you about Randy's and Melinda's ghosts?"

"He mentioned that the domestic help believed in them," Megan replied, cautious that she reveal nothing that might put a psychological weapon in this man's hands and not sure why she felt that way.

Paul Gorman closed his eyes momentarily, then opened his eyes to look down at Megan. His expression spoke of old pain and regret. "Jimmy believes that the ghosts walk. The first time he spent the night with Dad after the suicide, he woke up screaming in the middle of the night. He claimed to hear Randy walking up and down the stone hall upstairs. Randy always wore boots, and the sound of his footsteps was very distinctive, very loud on these stone floors. I used to tease him that he could never creep up on someone unawares. Jimmy still occasionally spends a night here, and he sleeps in an adjoining bedroom to Dad's, the only place he feels safe upstairs. Occasionally Dad will still hear him scream out to Randy. "Shut up, Randy! Quit walking!" At least, that's what Dad hears him say, or perhaps I should say, that's as much as Dad will tell me."

Megan felt shivers run up her spine, and not because the entry hall was cold as the Arctic Circle. "Do you think your father is lying to you?"

Paul shook head. "No, but I don't think he tells me everything, either. Jimmy is very fragile, Doctor Clark, and although I know I have no control over you, I wish you would be very circumspect when questioning Jimmy. I don't know if his mother could live through another of Jimmy's breakdowns, and I'm not sure Jimmy could, either. He spends entirely too much time thinking of his brother's suicide."

"And you think Jimmy might also commit suicide?" asked Megan.

Paul Gorman hesitated, looking pensive before answering. "I don't know, Doctor Clark, but I think it's a possibility."

In the backseat of Herb's BMW on the way home, Megan wondered why, during Jimmy Gorman's "intensive therapy," no one reassured him that his anger at Randy's suicide was a normal response and nothing to beat himself up about. Just exactly what did Jimmy Gorman's intensive therapy involve, and how could she find out about it?

12

"Impact: The force with which two lives can come together. Sometimes for evil, sometimes for good."

VOICE-OVER NARRATOR
Impact, 1949

I was anxious to see how Megan had recovered from her trip to Hill House, so I rushed over as soon as I saw her come home from work. Did I mention that she is an assistant reference librarian until she can get a job in her real field? Unlike Nancy Drew, Megan has no well-off lawyer father to pay her bills, so she has to work. She was late, and I was about to the nail-chewing stage when her black behemoth GMC pickup turned in her driveway and rolled to the detached garage at the back of her house. I was out of my house in a heartbeat, trotting over to her pickup, when I heard a peculiar sound, a *woof-woof* like that from a baby toy I remember my daughter having. You probably know the type I'm talking about: you point at a particular object, pull the string, and a recording says "the dog goes woof-woof" or "the duck goes quack-quack." The point is, something in Megan's pickup was going woof-woof. She opened the door, and a brown and black and white four-legged creature jumped out and hurled itself in my direction. Before I was able to react, the creature was upon me, and I mean that literally. It jumped up, putting its small paws on what would be my lap if I were sitting down. Unfortunately, its head, when propelled by leaping, was on a level with my testicles. Instantaneously I was kneeling on the grass clutching myself and hoping to control the nausea, while the creature was busily woofing in my face.

"Don't worry, Ryan," said Megan, picking up the small wiggling bundle. "He won't bite, and he doesn't give doggie kisses, either, but he does express his opinion by barking. I think he's telling you that you are supposed to pet him."

"What is that?" I gasped.

"This is Horatio Hornbeagle. I found him on the street on my way home from work. He is skin and bones and has no collar, so I assume he has been abandoned. I had to take him to the vet for shots before I brought him home. I didn't want Rembrandt exposed to anything."

I had my breath back and was considering getting up when the dog creature seized my hand in his teeth, rolled over on his back, and let go of my hand in such a way that it fell naturally on a mostly bald belly.

"He wants you to rub his tummy, Ryan. I've discovered that he is into tummy rubs in a big way."

"But he doesn't have any hair on his belly."

"The vet said that's because he's malnourished. As soon as I feed him a decent diet, his hair will grow back. Isn't that right, Horatio?" she asked in a gushy voice.

Megan is dog crazy and makes over every hairy, sloppy dog as if it were God's gift. I don't mean to say that I am antidog. I, too, love dogs, but they don't return the favor with the insane enthusiasm of Megan's. Megan's dogs are so enamored of her that they automatically assume an attack dog stance whenever they sense one of her species engaging in a mating dance with Megan as the object of the exercise. I haven't engaged in any such activity, but Rembrandt doesn't trust me not to, and he will undoubtedly infect this small, sparsely haired puppy with his suspicions. Rembrandt is that kind of dog.

"What do you think Rembrandt will do with a rival for your affections?"

She looked at me as if I had just asked a foolish question to which there was an obvious answer. "Beagles are pack animals, Ryan. Rembrandt will accept Horatio as a member of his pack, so long as Horatio remembers who is the alpha dog."

I looked at the small dog, a long, skinny pink tongue hanging out of his mouth in ecstasy as his goddess rubbed his tummy—er—belly. "You'll have to check the lost dog ads. Beagles are expensive dogs. No one would have simply abandoned him."

She continued her ministrations to the dog's belly. "Yes, someone would. Horatio has a heart murmur and he had an epileptic seizure in the vet's office. A breeder couldn't show him, breed him, or sell him, so he was no good to anyone but me. I don't care if he's a show dog or not as long as he's lovable."

I raised myself to my knees, leaned over, and kissed her. What else could I do?

Horatio didn't growl at me, so I scratched him behind his ears.

"Come over after you introduce Horatio to Rembrandt and the fur has settled," I said, somewhat breathless after the lengthy kiss. I wasn't absolutely sure, but I think that Megan is participating in our kisses. I don't mean that she's wrapping her arms around me and melting against my manly chest, but she's not giving me those odd looks, either. "I'll mix up a pitcher of margaritas and we'll celebrate the remains of the day."

She looked a little dazed but still in command of herself as she shook her head. "No alcohol, Ryan. We have an appointment with former Lieutenant Roberts tonight, and I want us both to be clearheaded."

Former Lieutenant Ray Roberts lived two blocks from the A. D. Payne house in a craftsman style cottage which had been maintained with loving care. Roberts even owned an original Morris chair, not one of these modern rip-offs. I know because I found the furniture maker's label. Naturally I got caught snooping.

"It belonged to my father."

I leaped to my feet so fast I was lightheaded. "I've always like the arts and crafts movement in American architecture and furniture making," I mumbled as an excuse for being caught on my hands and knees examining his property like a burglar casing the joint.

"I inherited this cottage from my father, and well, my wife was dead, and our furniture was that sixties stuff that I never thought was very comfortable, so I gave most of it to Goodwill, and took over what I liked of my father's, bought a few things, and hey, I'm happy."

He waved us toward a couch, served us cold lemonade, and settled back in his Morris chair. His remaining hair was a combination brown and gray and rimmed his head in a neatly trimmed fringe, and he wore a mustache and goatee, which I noticed he smoothed whenever he was thinking about his answer to one of Megan's questions. He probably weighed ten pounds more than what he did when he was with the police, and his face had all the lines and grooves expected of a man nearing seventy. To my mind, he wore them proudly.

"So, Doctor Clark, you told me over the phone that

Bruce Gorman hired you to investigate Melinda Gorman's murder and Randy's suicide. Is that right?"

"Yes, and please call me Megan. Of course, Bruce Gorman wants us to find the outsider who killed Melinda, but I warned him that the probable murderer was a member of his own family. I think he finally admitted that my scenario was the most likely. I—and Murder by the Yard Reading Circle—have carte blanche to investigate. Herb Jackson, the attorney in our group, and Ryan and I were at the Gorman home yesterday. I questioned the Gormans and got some interesting answers to my questions."

"If you got anything out of the Gormans, you did better than me, Megan. They all had ice water running in their veins, except for Jimmy, and he was just a kid. And Randy, of course, but I always had a hard time thinking of Randy as a Gorman. I used to wonder if he was switched at birth."

"Why do you say that?" asked Megan, sitting on the edge of the couch to get closer to the lieutenant. I hoped she didn't slide off and bruise her tail bone.

"Because he was such a sensitive kid, and I don't mean sensitive like it's used today. You know, getting in touch with your feminine side and so forth. I mean he was open to people. That's why toward the end of the investigation, or the end as far as I was concerned, I just couldn't see him killing his wife. But I could see him putting that cushion under her head so she'd be more comfortable like he said in his first statement. That's the kind of thing he'd do. Would he hit his wife with a pool cue, then strangle her with her own belt? I wouldn't bet the farm on it." Roberts stopped and sipped his lemonade, his face placid. "But I've been fooled before. Maybe he fooled me."

"Did you know Jimmy Gorman had a nervous breakdown after Randy's suicide?" asked Megan.

Ray Roberts smoothed his mustache. "I had heard his father had him committed. I was a little surprised by it. I always figured Jimmy to be the toughest of the Gormans without being the coldest."

"He believes that Randy walks the upstairs hall. Supposedly, he hears his footsteps on the limestone. And the help, a cook, told Jimmy that Melinda haunted the gazebo. I didn't get the cook's name, but I plan on getting a list of the domestic help, along with their addresses and phone numbers."

"Won't do you any good, Megan," said Roberts. "All the domestic help who were in that house that night are dead."

"All of them?" gasped Megan.

"All of them except the gardener, Roosevelt Wilson, and he wasn't there that night. So, far as I know, he's still alive, but he's not talking. At least, he wasn't then, and I don't think time will have changed him any. I never saw a man as scared as that one. Once Earl Washington, the former butler, was shot, and Pearl Hutchins, the cook, got hold of a bad jar of home-canned green beans, I don't think holding Roosevelt's feet to the fire would have made him talk. The final blow was the little maid, Jenny something—I can't remember her last name—being beaten to death and dumped in an alley late one Saturday night couple of weeks after the murder. Jenny was helping Earl Washington serve dinner that night, then helped Pearl clean up the kitchen. Have you read the statements, Megan?"

"Lieutenant Jerry Carr won't let us read the statements. He says he doesn't want us disclosing any details to the suspects, and as I understand it, you believed all the Gormans were suspects."

"Far as I was concerned, they were—even the women. Once your victim is unconscious, it doesn't take much strength to strangle her with a ligature. Deanne or Michele Gorman could have done it. They were strong, athletic women. For that matter, so was Melinda's mother. Not that I ever considered her a real serious suspect, but you got to remember that mothers kill their children all the time, but they usually do it when the children are babies. Getting back to the statements, I'm not surprised the lieutenant wouldn't let you read them. Jerry Carr called me yesterday, urging me not to talk to you. He said that you and the reading circle were amateurs with too much time on your hands. If he had dared, I think the lieutenant would have threatened me with interfering with a police investigation if I talked to you. His whole attitude stuck in my craw, Megan. The police haven't done anything in the twenty years since I quit, and they won't do anything in the next twenty years unless somebody shames them into it. If you can find out something, more power to you, and I say that even though it goes against the grain. I was a police officer and you're an amateur, and when I was still on the force I wouldn't have given you the time of day. Or maybe I would. In a case like the Gorman murder I might have done almost anything to break it open. So you just ask all the questions you want and I'll answer as best I can. I'll even give you my field diary if you want."

"You found it then, Lieutenant Roberts? When I talked to you on the phone you said you'd have to look for it," said Megan, with what I'm ashamed to say was a greedy look on her face. I am becoming more and more concerned about her absorption in these murder cases. It isn't healthy.

"Oh, I knew where it was all the time, right in my filing cabinet under G for Gorman. All my papers that I felt I could get away with taking, I took. I haven't forgotten the Gorman case in the past twenty years, and I doubt I will in the next twenty years—if I last that long. Every once in a while I get out my field diary, sketches of the scene I drew from memory, and summaries of the statements, again from memory, and look over everything one more time. I keep hoping that I'll see something new, but I haven't. But to answer your question, I wasn't going to tell you anything until I took your measure for myself instead of depending on Lieutenant Carr's opinion.

"Why did you resign, Lieutenant Roberts—if I'm not offending you?" asked Megan, setting her lemonade down to take a notebook and pen from her purse.

Roberts smoothed his mustache and goatee. "Uncertainty, Megan, it was uncertainty that made me turn in my badge. For the first time in my career, I was uncertain about the identity of the murderer. Any decent cop can almost smell the guilty party in a domestic murder, and that's all the Gorman case is, despite all the money: a domestic murder. Randy and Melinda Gorman were two people who probably didn't belong together, trying to make it despite that fact, and they stirred up feelings like stirring up the mud at the bottom of a pond. But I couldn't figure out who the guilty party was. By the end of the investigation—meaning when I retired, because the investigation pretty well ended at that point—I was as uncertain as I was when the call first came in. I couldn't clear Randy by the evidence, and gut feelings don't count unless you can back them up with hard ev-

idence the DA can take to court. But I couldn't clear
anybody else, either. Of course, part of the problem is
that the old man, Bruce Gorman that would be, was
hollering that the killer sneaked onto the property and
walloped Melinda Gorman for the hell of it, and nearly
from the first, all the Gormans were singing that song.
It didn't do no good to point out the pool cue came from
Bruce Gorman's rec room—only I reckon you call it a
billiard room when it's as fancy as that one is—Bruce
Gorman wasn't listening. He was frantic that his grandson was innocent and called in so many lawyers that
you could practically hear them slithering from room to
room. Gorman even hired private detectives—"

"Just like Beal Sneed," interrupted Megan. "Beal
Sneed hired the Pinkertons to find his wife when she ran
away with Al Boyce."

"I heard tell about that case. Anyhow, maybe the
Pinkertons had more luck tracking down Lena Sneed
than the fancy detectives had with the Gorman case.
They told old man Gorman that it was an inside job, but
that they didn't know who the guilty party was. Gorman
fired them. Didn't pay them either, and got himself sued.
That man was dead set on his family being innocent.
But all my work, all the fancy detectives, it all boiled
down to one thing: I don't know who killed that little
girl, and that's the truth."

"What about the butler and the maid? It seems too
coincidental that both would be murdered within weeks
of Melinda's death."

"Three, Megan, all three were murdered. Pearl's bad
green beans turned out to be seasoned with botulism."

"Botulism!" I exclaimed. "That was some sloppy
home canning. How the devil did botulism end up in her
green beans?"

Ray Roberts looked at me and raised one eyebrow. "Now, that's a real good question, son, a real good question. And it isn't easy to answer, seeing as how the lid to the jar was gone. I had my men looking through garbage until I thought I might have a revolt on my hands. Never did find that lid—and I should have."

"You're saying that the Gormans—or at least one of the Gormans—is responsible for the murders of all three people?" asked Megan, an incredulous expression on her face.

"No wonder Deanne got so upset with you last night, Megan," I said, feeling a mild hysteria about to set in. "The Gormans really *do* murder the help."

13

"You can't just go round killing people whenever the notion strikes you. It's not feasible."

ELISHA COOK, JR.
(henchman Marty Waterman) to Lawrence Tierney
(killer Sam Wild),
Born to Kill aka Deadlier Than the Male, 1947

"I never could prove that," said Roberts. "God knows I tried, but I never got very far."

"Everybody have foolproof alibis?" Ryan asked, a use of the vernacular that only proved he had been watching films noir again, although Megan had to admit that it was a good question.

"That's the puzzle about it," said Roberts. "Technically, everybody had an alibi in that they alibied each other, which means that if you're the suspicious sort— like me—you don't believe anybody's alibi. The problem is that you can't prove somebody guilty just because their alibi isn't worth a damn, any more than you can prove them guilty if they don't have one at all. In other words, if I couldn't prove you were in a particular place at a particular time committing a murder, I can't arrest you just because you don't have an alibi. I can look at you hard, but I can't arrest you. That's the way these things work."

"But your gut feeling is that one of the Gormans killed

all three people?" Megan asked, chills running up and down her back just as they had at the Gorman mansion.

The angry expression in Lieutenant Roberts's faded blue eyes would be enough to stop a felon in his tracks. "I damn well know one of them did it! I don't believe in coincidences like three witnesses murdered in less than two weeks. And I investigated those murders right, left, and center, and the more I investigated, the worse it got. It turns out Earl Washington owed money on some gambling debts, and since gambling is illegal, the man who held his note wasn't likely to use an ordinary collection agency. Still, I don't think Earl would have been killed for five hundred dollars. But there was no way to be sure. And little Jenny, the maid, was playing two men off against one another, and that's a sure way for a woman to get herself in trouble. We tried to find the two men, but they both left town, and the police never could track them down. You ask me, they got paid to leave town, but I couldn't prove it."

"What about examining the Gormans's bank accounts for withdrawals?" asked Megan. "There's always a paper trail."

Ray Roberts rubbed his hand over his bald head and smiled at Megan. "I can tell you're not a lawyer, and I'm betting you didn't run that question by the lawyer in your group, or he would have told you the answer. No probable cause. I couldn't go before a judge and tell him that my gut told me that one of the Gormans was killing people, and I wanted a look at his bank account. Now, mind you, the judge might have agreed with my gut, but the law don't let you look at personal bank accounts just on the off chance that you might find something."

"What about the cook, Pearl? Don't tell me that

wasn't a clear case of murder," said Megan.

"Maybe, maybe not. It turns out that those green beans were canned by Pearl at the Gorman ranch, that being where the vegetable garden was, and the whole batch canned at the same time had botulism. The only thing that determined that Pearl's death was murder was that I had the good sense to look real careful at the lids of the rest of the batch. Somebody shoved a needle through the rubber seal on those jars and injected botulism. We found the hole in the rubber seals on all the jars. Of course, that made it look like somebody was out to kill the Gormans. And sure enough, there was a ranch hand with a grudge who had been fired a couple of weeks before. Of course, we never found the ranch hand, either. Another one of those disappearing witnesses."

"It's all so convenient, isn't it?" asked Megan.

"Real convenient—and I don't believe in convenient any more than I do coincidence—not in a murder investigation," said Roberts, his bristly gray eyebrows nearly meeting as he frowned.

"I guess I should ask you about your field notes and your summaries of the statements," said Megan. "Just give me a minute to warm up. It seems to be getting cold awfully early this year, don't you think?"

"It ain't the weather; it's the Gormans, and I suspect you know that. Tell you something else, don't try to deny evil by putting it down to the temperature. I got a theory that evil drains warmth and life out of the air. Hell isn't fire and brimstone, it's cold so bad that it nearly freezes you to death, but not quite. That's what the Vikings believed Hell was like, and after meeting the Gormans, I agree with the Vikings."

He leaned forward in his Morris chair, his expression earnest, staring at Megan until she shifted on the couch and avoided his eyes. He was so intense, and Megan didn't want to hear what he was going to say. "What I'm trying to tell you, Megan, is that you've got to believe that evil exists. If you don't believe that, you're in danger."

"She's in danger anyway," said Ryan, reaching for Megan's hands to warm them. "She doesn't have any business messing around with an old murder case, particularly one where conservatively, five people died."

"You got a reason for saying 'conservatively,' " asked Roberts.

"It seems to me that three missing witnesses is too convenient."

Megan glanced at Ryan, uncertain how she felt about his sudden assertiveness. He didn't know anything about solving mysteries, real or fictional, so why the interest in this one! She wasn't sure but that she wouldn't rather have him dragging his feet and complaining. But what did that say about her? That she wanted to be the one in charge with Ryan playing a submissive role? What an awful kind of attitude that would be. And what about that kiss this afternoon? It seemed to her that Ryan was being awfully free with his kisses. And how did she feel about that? She didn't know, and with a murder—or maybe eight murders waiting to be solved, she would simply have to think about it tomorrow.

"Wait a minute, Lieutenant Roberts, what did you just say?" She noticed Ryan's raised eyebrow. She hated to admit she hadn't been paying attention, but she hadn't.

"I was just telling young Ryan here that he hit the nail on the head. I always wondered what I'd find if I had been able to get a search warrant and go over the Gorman ranch inch by inch. I think I would have found three fresh graves, two for Jenny's missing boyfriends and one for the disgruntled ranch hand. But I didn't have probable cause to ask to search the whole one hundred and ten sections any more than I had cause to look at the Gorman bank accounts. That's the secret of getting away with murder: Make sure the cops don't have probable cause to get a search warrant for a damn thing. You know I never got a search warrant for the Gorman mansion, just the grounds around the murder scene and Randy's and Melinda's bedroom. That was it, that was all I could talk a judge into giving me."

"Did you find anything suspicious?" asked Megan.

"Not a damn thing."

"Tell me what the Gormans said in their statements—the best you can remember."

"First of all, Tommy Mitchell was drunker than a skunk, but I bet someone already told you that."

"Jake was kind enough to share that information," said Megan.

"Jake the snake. That's what I always called him to myself 'cause he was such cold, slick galoot. Well, old Jake said he didn't leave the room except to go to the bathroom. Paul left the room to give orders to Earl, the butler, about snacks and drinks. He might have been gone ten minutes, he might have been gone five. Who knows? Earl didn't. He just said Paul gave orders and left the kitchen. Jake and Randy Gorman were engaged in a hot pool game, and weren't paying any attention."

"Jake said that Randy left the room once with his pool cue and once without it."

"He did? That's news to me. He never told me anything like that. He said Randy left the room when he won the pool game to look for Melinda."

"How did he know to look in the gazebo?" asked Ryan. "You know, that's always been a stumbling block for me. If he didn't kill his wife, how did he know where to look for her?"

"I never got an answer for that question," said Roberts, getting out of his chair to pour more lemonade.

"It's obvious," said Megan. "Someone told him."

"But who?" asked Roberts. "Nobody mentioned telling Randy that his wife was in the gazebo."

"Of course not," said Megan, "because that would raise the question of how did that particular person know if he—or she—hadn't arranged to meet Melinda there."

"What did Trent have to say for himself?" asked Ryan, another intrusion into the investigation that shocked Megan. Ryan didn't believe in amateur sleuths. What was he doing asking questions?

"He was playing bridge and only got up to see about refreshments."

"No wonder Earl was murdered," said Megan. "He was in the position to know who was wandering around, and a comparison between his estimation of the time and the estimation by either Janice at the bridge game or Tommy Mitchell in the billiard room would destroy some alibis."

"Except Tommy was drunk," Ryan pointed out. "Time wouldn't mean much to him.

"That's another interesting factor," said Megan. "Tommy Mitchell, the victim's brother, who should have been in a position to support or destroy alibis, is drunk. I find it puzzling that Bruce Gorman would have allowed so much liquor served to Tommy at dinner that he was stumbling drunk by the end of the meal. Another thing, Lieutenant Roberts. Did your investigation turn up evidence that Melinda was promiscuous? Michele Gorman called her a slut, and went into some detail about her behavior at Gorman Oil."

"One of the mantras that Paul Gorman chanted to support the idea of an outsider was that Melinda must have had a lover. He was ignoring the pool cue, but so did every other Gorman. Did she have a lover? According to the other secretaries, yes, she was keeping close company with somebody before she was married, and it wasn't Randy Gorman, but for once a woman kept a secret. The secretaries guessed every one of the Gormans, and no more had any proof to back up their gossip than the man in the moon."

"What about Randy? What did he say in his statement?" asked Megan, scooting even closer to the edge of the couch and sitting with her pen poised to write.

"That he went hunting for his wife and found her dead in the gazebo. Of course, the Gorman lawyers got there about as quickly as the police, and Bruce Gorman had already told Randy not to say anything more than those two facts. Oh, he did say he hadn't taken a pool cue to the gazebo. That was it, and a year later, that was still it. To tell you the truth, that boy was hysterical that night. Anything I got out of him probably would have been inadmissible, but I didn't get anything out of him. Then he was dead, and the case was over."

"Did you talk to him that day?" asked Megan, her pen still poised but nothing written on her notebook. Lieutenant Roberts had little more information than she.

"No, I hadn't talked to him. I hadn't talked to him in a week. There wasn't any point in it. He was going to tell me the same thing, and the rest of the Gormans were going to tell me the same thing, and there were no witnesses left to dispute their versions.

"Who did talk to Randy that day?" asked Megan.

Roberts pursed his lips as he thought. "Jimmy Gorman, and the boy's grandpa, Bruce Gorman, his dad,

Paul. His mother was there around noon, pleading for Randy to move back home, according to her. Jake the snake was there in the morning, but not in the afternoon at the time of the suicide. Trent came with Jake, and they both left at the same time. What did they say to Randy? I have no idea. They said they just dropped by to see how he was and ask if he wanted to go to dinner that night. You can bet your bottom dollar that they were lying about the topic of conversation, but I couldn't prove it. Randy Gorman, the only one who could dispute them, was dead, and by the evening of that next day, I had resigned. My uncertainty had killed that boy, and I knew I'd never be worth a damn as a cop again."

Megan didn't know what to say to dispute Roberts's statement. She had never been a cop, but she suspected that once one's confidence was gone, then self-doubt set in, and there was no going back. "Can we see your file, Lieutenant? Maybe you didn't do such a bad job as you think."

"Yeah, I did, Megan, but you're welcome to the file. God knows, I haven't been able to do anything with it in twenty years. Maybe a new pair of eyes will see something I've been missing. I'm sorta like Bruce Gorman. I'd like to know the answer before I die."

The old officer slowly got up from his Morris chair, looking every bit of his age. Megan thought it was as if talking about the Gorman case drained away what remained of his youth. He motioned them to follow as he walked with cramped step into a small room off the living area. The room held an old rolltop desk, a wall of bookshelves that held more file boxes than books, and two filing cabinets. Roberts went directly to the shelves and pulled out two thick file boxes and handed them to Megan.

"This is what records I have on the Gorman case. Some papers are summaries of statements like I told you, but some are copies of the real McCoy, depending on what I had time to do. When word came in about Randy's suicide, I knew I was quitting the force, but I couldn't bring myself to quit the case, so I copied what I could and summarized from memory what I couldn't copy. What you've got in your hands is the complete case file of the Gorman murder and suicide as best I could reconstruct it."

He hesitated a moment as if he was holding an internal debate, then shrugged his shoulders as though he had come to a decision. "If there comes a time you might need me, Megan, just give me a holler. I'm still licensed to carry, and it strikes me that you might need someone watching your back."

Distracted, Megan nodded her head. Then, unable to wait a single minute longer, she sat the file boxes on the desk and delved into the first one. It held statements filed alphabetically by name, crime scene reports, and a field notebook. The second file box held the autopsy report, reports on such hard evidence as the ligature, blood analysis, further statements, and a folder labeled "Miscellaneous." Megan pulled it out and opened it. She had never been able to resist any file, box, drawer, etc., filled with miscellaneous papers. You never knew what you might find.

She gasped. "Oh, my God!"

"What?" demanded Roberts, stepping to her side and looking over her shoulder. "That's just the bridge scorecard. I don't even know why it's in there except I was picking up everything that night. It's no good, though, because I didn't have a search warrant, so I just dropped it in the miscellaneous file."

Megan whirled to look at him. "My God, Lieutenant Roberts, don't you know what this is? It's the blueprint of who was dummy and when, who could leave the table and when. All I need to know is who got the bid on the first hand, and who was his or her partner. It's an alibi card, or rather it tells us who needed an alibi."

TRAGIC LOVE TRIANGLE:
THE BOYCE-SNEED FEUD

"Brown-beared, brown-suited, brown-cravated and munching a soggy and partially smoked brown Havana, John Beal Sneed, charged with the murder of Al G. Boyce, the son of previously murdered Colonel A. G. Boyce, entered the Forty-seventh district court room yesterday afternoon at the beginning of the habeas corpus hearing which will give or deny him liberty on bail." Thus did the *Amarillo Daily News* of September 23, 1912, report the appearance of John Beal Sneed in a courtroom crowded by the finest ladies and gentlemen of Amarillo society. It was the scandal of the new century, and indeed, never surpassed for pure drama by any other murder case in the following eighty-nine years. A love triangle, a double murder, acquittal in both cases, and a family feud that lasted nearly fifty years, until the last of the Boyce family either moved or died, no case in Texas Panhandle history equaled the Boyce-Sneed feud and its bloody results. As childhood friends, Lena Synder, Beal Sneed, and Al Boyce were inseparable. At Georgetown University near Austin, both men courted her. Lena married Beal Sneed and for the next twelve years seemed content, if not precisely happy. Two girls were born to the marriage, the couple lived in a luxurious home, and were members of Amarillo high society as it existed then. Beal Sneed traveled a great deal as a cattle buyer, being unsuccessful in making a living in his profession of law. He thus left Lena alone with their two girls for lengthy periods, but many women were wives of cattle buyers who left them alone without becoming the focus of scandal and murder. Indeed, Beal Sneed was not the first man to learn his wife had found another interest, but he differed in that instead of divorcing his straying spouse as most men would do, he shot the lover and the lover's father, stood trial for two murders, and kept his wife. During the hearing in Amarillo in September, 1912, two ladies who kept a boarding house in Dallas where the Sneeds had stayed after the first murder, testified that Lena Sneed swore that Al Boyce was the love of her life, and she would never love again. Perhaps that was true. The relations between Lena and Beal Sneed during the rest of their lives were seldom spoken of, and remain a matter left to the imagination, but one can hardly believe that the marriage was happy. The matters closest to the hearts of Lena and Beal Sneed were the matters they could not mention.

The sordid tragedy that was the Boyce-Sneed feud began, according to Beal Sneed's testimony at the habeas corpus hearing, the previous year when Beal returned from a business trip and went home for lunch. "When I arrived, she sent the children into dinner and said, 'I have something to tell you.' I said, 'all right, what is it?' She said, 'Come out on the gallery.' We sat on the swing on the front gallery and she blatantly proceeded to tell me of her love for Al Boyce."

Beal Sneed claims to be ignorant of his wife's affair with Al Boyce, but all of Amarillo, from society dames to their maids knew about it, so either he was extraordinarily naive, or easily fooled. After his wife's confession, he placed her in an sanatarium in Fort Worth for treatment of "moral insanity." With Al Boyce's help,

Lena escaped the sanatarium and the two lovers fled to Canada and were finally tracked down in Winnipeg. According to informed sources, Beal Sneed hired the Pinkertons to find his wife, but was also aided by a Canadian attorney. At any rate, Lena was taken back to New Mexico by her father, Tom Synder, one assumes to think over her actions. Beal Sneed in the meantime filed charges against Al Boyce for abduction. Sneed lost his case in early January, 1912, but Colonel A. G. Boyce, Al Boyce's father, holding court in the lobby of the just completed Metropolitan Hotel in Fort Worth, was very outspoken about Sneed's inability to hold onto his wife. To a man smarting from the humiliation of his wife's preferring another man, the colonel's words were like waving a red flag at an already very angry bull. Beal Sneed shot at the colonel six times with a .38 revolver, missing only once. Sneed was tried for murder, his defense being that the colonel had assisted his son in the breakup of the Sneed marriage. The jury deadlocked at seven to five for acquittal, and Sneed was free on bond, and the next act in this deadly drama was only months away.

It was a hot September, and one imagines that Beal Sneed found his newly hirsute face itched in the enclosed heat of the modest shotgun cottage owned by Charlie Green at 803 Polk Street, just across the street from the First Methodist Church. A shotgun cottage is one in which the rooms are in a straight line opening one into the other, which affords little privacy. But privacy wasn't what Beal Sneed sought that September of 1912; rather it was a hiding place in which to wait for Al G. Boyce to walk down Polk Street unaccompanied by his brothers. The Boyces were fine shots with revolvers or rifles; Beal Sneed was an indifferent shot despite lessons from a tenant farmer named B. B. Epting. For that reason he chose as his weapon a double-barreled shotgun. It was difficult to miss if you got close enough to your victim, and Sneed intended to be very close.

The weeks—at least two and perhaps three, depending on the sources consulted—passed slowly while Sneed sweated under his newly grown beard, filthy bib overalls of heavy denim, and thick-soled worker's boots, so different from his usual attire. His beard was dyed black, and his receding reddish hair was completely hidden under a black hat. No one would recognize Beal Sneed, so different was he from the heavyset, clean-shaven man Amarillo knew.

Boyce was tall, slender with thick hair, a handsome man and attractive to the ladies, or at least one lady in particular: Lena Sneed. Heavyset Beal Sneed would be overlooked by the ladies if dashing Al Boyce was in the room. How much of Sneed's humiliation and his determination that Al Boyce would not have Lena depended upon his feelings that Boyce was the handsome prince while he was the homely frog cannot be known, but as Beal sat in front of the window in that shotgun house waiting for Boyce, he must have brooded on his physical inferiority to Boyce. If he, Sneed, had been the handsome one, son of the legendary manager of the XIT, largest ranch in the world, would his wife have strayed? Did Lena marry him only because Al Boyce moved to the XIT from Georgetown before proposing? Was he second choice, second rate? As the afternoon sun shone down on the cottage, heating its interior to a sweating temperature, such thoughts must have stirred his ire to the point that no one would be able to talk him out of his vengeance. Not that there is much evidence that anyone tried. Sneed's father could not. He was dead months after Boyce's father, slain by a tenant farmer whom Sneed believed was "put up to it" by the Boyces. It was not true, but Beal Sneed was beyond logic as he practiced his shooting and waited for Al Boyce to return to Amarillo. The town waited also, knowing that a showdown between Beal Sneed and Al Boyce was coming, but knowing there was little anyone could do to stop it. The rage and humiliation, the arrogance, and the ideal of frontier justice would blend together to create a tragedy in many acts written in blood.

The tragedy began with Act One: the confrontation between Beal and Lena Sneed which ended in her incarceration, and her escape with her lover to Canada. The last act began on Saturday morning, September 14, 1912, a beautiful fall day with a light wind from the southwest, when an immaculately dressed Al Boyce left his home at 1102 Polk, just two blocks from the First Methodist Church, then at 800 Polk. He was alone. He exchanged greetings with the Dr. Ernest E. Robinson, minister of the Methodist church, who was on his way home with the week's groceries, and continued down Polk on his way to his father's bank. At last, the final scene. Beal Sneed grasps his shotgun, holding it close to his leg so it was not obvious. He leaves the shotgun cottage and crosses the street, then begins to walk toward Al Boyce, closer and closer to Al Boyce, handsome Al Boyce who destroyed his home and stole away his wife's love. He watches Boyce's eyes, as every shootist tells you to do, as the eyes will give away intent, but Al Boyce had no intent to murder that day—or perhaps any day—as all the killing done during the feud was done by Beal Sneed. Al Boyce only wanted Lena Sneed, not blood. But it was blood he got instead as Beal Sneed leveled his shotgun and emptied both barrels into Al Boyce, reloaded and shot him a third time, leaving him bleeding to death on the steps of the First Methodist Church. Sneed turned and walked down Polk Street toward the courthouse where he would turn himself in. According to her biographer, Laurie Lisle, on the next block, at 706 Polk, in the Magnolia Hotel, Georgia O'Keeffe was playing dominoes with other residents when she heard three shots. She ran to the door and asked a man in bib overalls "What's the trouble?" The man answered, "Nothing. I killed him."

Beal Sneed was later acquitted of the murder of Al Boyce. In the words of the jury foreman, J. D. Crane, "The best answer is because this is Texas. We believe in Texas a man has the right and the obligation to safeguard the honor of his home, even if he must kill the person responsible."

Drs. Stevens and Clark on the circumstances of the Boyce-Sneed feud.

14

*"Every night I dream I read somewhere about a—
about a kind of doctor. A psych-something. You tell
your dream, you don't have to dream it anymore."*

ALAN LADD
(hired killer Philip Raven),
This Gun For Hire, 1942

"You've got the scorecard, Megan," I said in what I already knew by Megan's clenched teeth would be a futile argument. "I don't suppose it would do any good for me to suggest that you take it to Jerry Carr and point out its importance?"

"No, it wouldn't do any good at all, so don't waste your breath."

I cleared my throat, risked a quick glance at her square jaw and pursed lips, and thought I might as well stay the course as long as I was in the argument. I don't want anybody to ever say that I'm a quitter. "He's the cop. He can question the four bridge players and discover who left the table."

Megan turned off Sixth Street onto Virginia and parked in front of a two-story, frame duplex that dated from at least the twenties. She turned off the ignition and looked at me with that patient expression on her face that tells me I've made a monumentally stupid remark. "There are all kinds of alibis, Ryan, and who left when is not the most important information I learned from the scorecard. According to the *American Heritage Dictionary*, the second definition of alibi is *excuse*. Someone in that bridge game went down four tricks three times in a row. What is his or her excuse for such poor card playing? What is distracting the player from the game? More importantly, what happened to the distraction, because immediately after the last loss, the player in question made a four bid, a five bid, and a six bid. Just imagine Jerry Carr asking one of the Gormans why he or she went down four tricks twenty years ago. Jerry Carr never listened to me in either the first or the second case we solved, so why should he listen now?"

It was a reasonable question. I wished I had a reasonable answer instead of admitting that Jerry Carr was a stubborn jerk some of the time. The problem is that Megan has never really forgiven him for accusing her of murder. Not that I care particularly, except at times like these when I want her to go to the police. I mean, I'm mature enough to put my jealousy of a younger man aside if it means Megan's welfare. Did I say jealousy? Yes, I did. I confess I've fallen in love with a woman nineteen years my junior, my oldest daughter's best friend, and I have a horror of being rejected in favor of a man her own age. I have a greater horror of making a fool of myself. But my greatest horror of all is that Megan will discover my feelings and try to let me down gently. Could anything be more horrible than that?

So I try to hide my feelings by acting as her best friend, her counselor, her companion—except when I succumb to temptation and kiss her, which only muddies the water—but so far she has not demanded the meaning of such intimacies. When she does, I don't know what I'll do. Probably lie.

"So you're determined to go ahead with this investigation regardless of the risk?"

"What risk? I'm not at any particular risk, Bruce Gorman is. All Murder by the Yard has agreed to do is investigate and turn over the results to Bruce Gorman. From the moment he knows our conclusions to the time he can get to his lawyer's office to write the guilty party out of his will, he's at risk."

I ran my hands through my hair. It's something I do when I'm frustrated, which mostly happens when I'm with Megan. "Conclusions? What conclusions?"

She looked at me as if I had just asked a silly question better suited to a seven-year-old. "Ryan, if I investigate a murder, I expect to come to the proper conclusion."

"How can you be so sure, when Lieutenant Roberts admitted he retired because he was uncertain of the murderer's identity, and Lieutenant Roberts had years of experience solving murder cases? Have you thought about that, Megan?"

She looked huffy, or as huffy as Megan can look, which is sort of like a baby chicken with its feathers all puffed out. "Of course I've thought of it, Ryan. I'm not an imbecile. But what I have in place of Lieutenant's Roberts's experience is the cooperation of Bruce Gorman, the freedom to ask questions without heed to the Miranda warning, and a very imaginative mind. Just look what I've already concluded about the bridge score card."

She had me there. That scorecard did seem to indicate that someone was not paying attention to the game. But her chances of actually coming to an accurate conclusion scared the bejesus out of me. "Did it occur to you that any conclusions that you arrive at will cost one of the Gorman heirs several million dollars? Don't you think that individual might be just a little pissed off at you?"

"Don't raise your voice, Ryan. It makes you appear hysterical." She grabbed her purse, which was the size of a small backpack, and opened her door. "Let's go see the Mitchells. Maybe Melinda's mother and brother can tell us more than just who partnered whom at the bridge game, and who got the bid in the opening hand."

If it weren't for the errand we were on, I would have enjoyed looking at the architecture of the old duplex. A hall, bisected by a wall separating it from the other side of the duplex, ran down one side from which the rooms opened, beginning with a living room, then dining room and large kitchen. To get from one room to another, it was necessary to step into the hall. I presumed the bedrooms and bath opened off a duplicate hall upstairs. For its time, the duplex was a luxurious home in an upper-middle-class neighborhood, but now it was a down-at-the-heels shelter in need of a new coat of paint inside and out.

Down at the heels also described Tommy Mitchell. Dressed in a white T-shirt that stretched over the beginnings of a fine beer belly, jeans that were not quite clean, and sporting a black-and-gray stubble that indicated he hadn't bothered to shave for our visit, he didn't appear to be anyone with whom I would enjoy a long afternoon's conversation. A man in his early forties still living with his mother, who so far as I could tell was in perfect health, spelled either a spoiled marriage with high child support payments or a wastrel who threw his money away on beer and pool and playing the lottery. If that statement makes me sound like a snob, so be it. I've never had any use for men who didn't practice self-reliance.

Janice Mitchell was a neatly groomed woman in her

early sixties but with a taste for blue eye shadow and heavy black mascara. Her eyes were medium blue and her lashes long and thick, so I could understand her emphasizing those features, but her heavy touch with the makeup made her look harsh. I suspected her eyes would be spectacular enough without makeup, and if her daughter inherited her mother's eyes, I began to understand men's fascination with Melinda Gorman. But then I only had Michele Gorman's word on that subject, and I didn't know how much of that disturbed woman's claims to believe.

"Tommy spent most of the morning down at the shop, and I didn't know if he would make it home in time for your visit," said Janice Mitchell, putting her hands together and squeezing them between her knees in a gesture of social discomfort. Suddenly I felt very sorry for this woman.

"Where do you work?" Megan asked Tommy, an expression of interest on her face that I knew was genuine. As an anthropologist, Megan finds every lifestyle and livelihood fascinating. As uncomfortable as it makes me to admit it, Megan is a much more democratic person than I.

Tommy responded by sitting up straighter and sucking in his gut. "At a machine shop down on Tenth. If it's any kind of a motor, we can work on it. Doesn't matter if it's lawn mowers or cars."

"That's a rare occupation these days," said Megan. "With all the specialties, it's good that someone is still capable of repairing motors of all kinds. I work on my truck if the repair is anything I can do myself." That did it. From that moment on, Megan Clark held Tommy Mitchell's heart in her small hands.

Janice Mitchell and I sat quietly while Megan and

Tommy spoke of wrenches and torque—whatever that is—and manifolds and carburetors and fuel injection. Have I ever mentioned that Megan owns her own tool kit and knows the name and function of every tool in it? Had she not been a paleopathologist, I'm sure she would have made a magnificent mechanic.

Finally, the talk of mechanics and motors tapered off, and Megan turned to Janice Mitchell. "I'm sorry you weren't at Bruce Gorman's the other night."

Janice Mitchell's blue eyes burned. "I haven't spoken to a Gorman in twenty years, and I don't intend to speak to one for the next twenty. I never believed that Randy killed Melinda, and I'll go to my grave not believing it. He loved my girl, loved her more than life itself, certainly loved her more than he loved that stuck-up witch of a mother of his. Did you hear how he defied her and moved in with his grandpa when she started pitching a fit about his marrying Melinda? Now, that's love when a boy will take the side of his wife over his family. And Randy did. And then I'm supposed to believe he killed her, and not just killed her, but strangled her? I saw her body before the police got there, her pretty face all swollen and purple, and her eyes bugging out and her tongue—I can't talk about how her tongue looked."

I shifted uncomfortably in my chair. I suspected that Janice Mitchell has recycled her daughter's death scene in her mind every day for twenty years. How could she not? How could she ever forget it?

"I haven't had a decent night's sleep since then," continued Janice Mitchell. "Tommy finally moved in with me when my nerves got so bad I couldn't work anymore."

She leaned over and grasped Megan's hands. "You

better hope you never see your daughter in such a fix. It kills a mother's life."

Tommy nodded solemnly. "There wasn't no help for it. I had to move in. Mom was falling to pieces."

I felt lower than a snake in a wagon rut. I was making all kinds of judgments about Tommy Mitchell, and all the time he was taking care of his mother. Here was another blighted family: mother an emotional wreck, son sacrificing his own independence to care for her. How much further harm would we see that started with Melinda Gorman's murder?

I glanced at Megan to see her swallow. She's a tenderhearted woman, and I know listening to the Mitchells must have been tearing her up.

"Tommy, do you think your sister was murdered because she married Randy Gorman?"

Tommy rubbed the stubble on his chin, and I saw the grease staining the cuticles and knuckles of his fingers. "I ain't never thought of it exactly like that, but yeah, I do. If she hadn't married Randy Gorman, she'd still be alive. But it wasn't Randy that killed her. I agree with Mom on that. Randy never held himself out as being better than the next person. It was one of them other Gormans that killed her. They didn't like it because a little girl from the poor part of town married into the rich bitch world. It was all right that she worked for Gorman Oil company, but don't step out of her place."

"Mrs. Mitchell, do you agree with Tommy?" asked Megan. "Do you think Melinda was killed because she didn't stay in her place?"

Janice Mitchell sat on the old, faded couch with tears running down her face. "Yes."

Megan took a deep breath, and I knew what was coming, knew there was no way to head her off. "Mrs. Mitchell, what was her place?"

The woman looked puzzled. "She was a secretary at Gorman Oil."

Megan took another deep breath, then plunged into the innuendo that surrounded Melinda Gorman. "Was she more than that, Mrs. Mitchell?"

Janice Mitchell stiffened, and she stared at Megan for a moment before looking away. "I don't know what you're talking about."

"You can't make them kind of remarks about Melinda!" shouted Tommy.

"What kind of remarks do you mean?"

"Talking about her like she was a whore!"

"I never called your sister that name, and I wouldn't ever do so," said Megan. "But what I'm asking goes to the heart of my investigation. It goes to the heart of a woman. Was Melinda more than a secretary to one of the Gorman men? Was she in love with one of the Gormans other than Randy? Did she betray a lover by marrying Randy?"

Tommy stumbled off the couch, his fists clenched. "You don't say another word about Melinda. Just get on out of here."

He didn't know Megan. She squared her shoulders and burrowed in like a mole, hunting for the truth. I got up and balled my fists, just in case, though. I figured I could take Tommy Mitchell.

"She wouldn't be killed just because she was a poor girl who married a wealthy man. Not even the Gormans would kill for that motive," said Megan.

I wasn't too sure of that. There wasn't much I'd put past the Gormans.

Janice Mitchell caught her son's hand and pulled him

back down on the couch, while Megan frowned me back into my chair. "Hush, Tommy, you don't know nothing about it."

He pulled his hand out of his mother's grasp. "Nothing about what, Mom? What don't I know about?"

"I think Miss Clark is right. I think Melinda was making up with somebody before Randy, but Randy was the one who would marry her, so she took up with him. You didn't live here, Tommy, you don't know the number of nights she'd leave and walk down the street to meet somebody. It got so I'd try to follow her, but she was watching, and she'd tear into me something terrible. She wanted out of here so bad, wanted things she'd never had before. This neighborhood is getting to be good again, what with all the hoop-de-la over Sixth Street being part of Route 66, but twenty years ago, it was a poor place to live. I was a widow and had a job down at one of the secondhand furniture stores on Sixth Street for minimum wage. They call themselves antique stores now, but not then. Melinda had a good job at Gorman Oil and could afford some real nice clothes and a new car, too. She was such a pretty girl, I didn't blame her for buying clothes and makeup and stuff. Looks don't last long, so you might as well make the most out of them while you can. And Melinda did. She landed herself Randy Gorman, but you're right, Miss Clark. I don't think he was the first Gorman she hooked."

"Mom, you're talking crazy. Melinda wasn't no street corner slut!" shouted Tommy Mitchell. I felt sorry for him. This was a hell of a thing to find out about your dead sister.

"Sit down and close your mouth, son. You're like all men. You get an idea in your head about a woman, and you don't see anything else. Melinda wanted to better herself, and I don't blame her. Who'd want to live poor all her life, making do from paycheck to paycheck? But Melinda didn't have much of a chance. Randy was away at college, so she didn't have a chance at him until it was too late. Somebody else already had his hooks in her, and he wasn't about to give her up."

"Like Beal Sneed," murmured Megan.

"I don't know him," said Janice Mitchell.

"No, you wouldn't. It happened years and years ago. Beal Sneed wouldn't give up his wife to another man and killed him over her."

Janice looked confused. "But my girl was the one who got killed."

"Of course," said Megan. "Her lover wasn't going to kill a member of his own family. He'd kill Melinda instead. But like Beal Sneed, he never let another man have her."

"That's one way to look at it, Miss Clark," agreed Janice Mitchell. "It might even be the only way."

"But who was it, Mrs. Mitchell?"

Janice Mitchell squeezed her hands together and looked frustrated. "I don't have any idea."

Megan turned her attention to the glowering Tommy Mitchell. "The Gormans said you were drunk that night."

He sat down heavily on the old couch as if he had lost the strength in his legs. "Yeah, I was, and I don't understand it. I don't remember having more than a couple of glasses of that fancy wine the Gormans served. I don't much like wine, and I was just drinking it to be polite. I sure didn't drink enough to get drunk."

He rubbed his face, and I caught sight of a tear. "If I hadn't been drunk, maybe I would have noticed something."

"Who poured the wine, Tommy?"

"That snooty black butler poured my second glass, but I don't know who poured the first. The glasses were full when we sat down. Real fancy, that dinner was, cards telling you where to sit and little bowls to wash your hands in."

"So anyone who wanted to slip something in your glass knew exactly where you would be sitting," said Megan.

"You mean like a Mickey Finn," I said.

Megan spared me a disapproving look but nodded her head. I wondered what I said wrong. Mickey Finn was the term used in the old detective movie I had watched the night before.

"Something like that. One glass of drugged wine was all it took," said Megan.

"That must be just what happened!" exclaimed Tommy Mitchell. "Those damn Gormans! Getting me drunk like that, so I couldn't protect my sister!"

Megan shook her head. "No, Tommy. Getting you drunk so you wouldn't notice who was leaving the billiard room and when."

"But I noticed some," protested Tommy. "Not much, but some. I never drank after them two glasses of wine, so I wasn't completely out of it. I was still on my feet."

"Who left?"

"Paul Gorman, then I saw Randy leave for a minute. That cousin, Jake Gorman, left, too, but I couldn't tell you how long any of them was gone, not without playing pool again. That might help me remember, if I was playing pool and I could kind of keep track by the way the game was going."

"We'll see what we can do about that," said Megan before turning her attention to Janice Mitchell again.

"About the bridge game, Mrs. Mitchell. Who was your partner?"

"Old Mr. Bruce Gorman. Michele Gorman was partners with her son."

Megan pulled the scorecard from her purse and handed it to Janice Mitchell. "Who went down four, five, and six tricks on successive hands?"

"That was Michele and Trent Gorman. I thought it was kind of funny because she bragged about how much bridge she played before we started the first rubber. Then she bid like an idiot. I doubled on all three hands. She played like an idiot, too. She didn't get her trumps in first of all, then she would take a trick with an ace when a jack would have done. This may be a poor neighborhood, but we know how to play bridge. I didn't understand what she was trying to do."

"Did Trent leave the room while he was dummy?"

Janice frowned. "I think he may have once."

"For how long?"

"I wasn't paying attention, but maybe for the whole hand."

"Did anything happen that turned things around? I mean, when did Michele go from bidding like an idiot to taking the bid and making seven?"

"She didn't. Trent took that bid."

"Did Michele leave the room while she was dummy?"

"Oh, yes. Both times."

"*Both* times?" asked Megan, her eyes opening wide.

Janice Mitchell nodded. "Yes. She was dummy on the six bid. Trent opened with one club and she jumped him to six. I never understood that, since she didn't have but two clubs in her hand, and they were low ones."

15

"Were you paying for the drinks, or was she paying for them?"
"I can say with pride I've never paid for anything in my life."

GENE TIERNEY
(gambler Poppy) to Victor Mature (her lover, Dr. Omar),
The Shanghai Gesture, 1940

Megan tapped her finger on the steering wheel while waiting for Ryan to squeeze himself into the passenger seat of her truck. When he was half turned toward her and belted in, she gestured toward the glove compartment. "Hand me my cell phone."

He looked startled. "Cell phone? I thought you hated cell phones."

"I do," she said, holding out her hand. "That's why I keep it turned off and locked in the glove compartment, but I couldn't ask Janice Mitchell to borrow her phone so I could call Bruce Gorman to find out if Melinda was making payments on her new car. I don't exactly want a dead girl's mother to know that I suspect her daughter had been given a new car by a man in exchange for sex."

"That's a harsh judgment, Megan, and there's no way for you to know that for sure."

"Unless Melinda Gorman saved her baby-sitting money for forty years, there's no way she could afford a new car without making payments."

"So you conclude Melinda Gorman's mysterious lover gave her the car?" asked Ryan as he handed her the phone. "You can't possibly know that. I don't know how you can even suspect it."

"Because she was trapped, Ryan, in a job that would never pay her enough to buy a car, nice new clothes, and get her out of her mother's duplex. She was vulnerable to a good offer. She was as trapped as Lena Sneed, and like Lena, she made a choice that turned out to be deadly."

"You don't know that either—that she wasn't paid enough," objected Ryan.

"Oh, Ryan, wake up and smell the coffee. She was a nineteen-year-old girl in 1980. She had no college education and probably very little experience beyond typing in high school. Remember, that was before every office had a computer and every school taught computer science. I would be surprised if she made much more than minimum wage as a clerk-typist."

"But Bruce Gorman said she was his private secretary."

Megan pursed her lips as she thought. "He did, didn't he? Well, maybe he was the mysterious lover. He would have been in his midsixties in 1980. It wouldn't be the first time an old geezer was chasing a girl young enough to be, well, be his granddaughter. Sometimes men are disgusting."

She noticed Ryan wincing and wondered if his back hurt. The way he had to scrunch up on the passenger side of her bench seat would make any tall man's back hurt. She ought to let him drive, bless his heart, so he could move the seat back to a comfortable distance from the steering wheel.

She opened the door and slid out, came around, and opened the passenger door. "You drive, Ryan."

"Why? You never let anybody drive this mammoth beast."

She patted his cheek. "You're special. Besides, I have to call Bruce Gorman, and I hate to see people driving down the street and talking on their cell phones. It's dangerous."

Ryan slid over and eased the seat back as far as it would go. "In that case I'll drive—as long as you're not doing me a favor because you think I'm too old to fold myself up enough to sit on the passenger seat."

Megan looked at him in surprise. "Old? What's old got to do with anything? You've been obsessing on age lately, Ryan, and you need to stop it. It's bad for your emotional health."

She dialed a number, then turned the phone off before it had a chance to ring. "I've changed my mind. This needs to be done in person, so I can watch his face. Take me to the Gorman mansion, Jeeves."

"Jeeves was a valet in the P. G. Wodehouse novels," muttered Ryan.

"I never read them. I was using the name Jeeves generically as that of a chauffeur or servant."

"He was always getting his employer, Bertie Wooster—who was very empty-headed—out of difficulties."

"Is that so?"

"Jeeves had more success than I do, since I can't convince you to leave the Gorman case alone. I'll just trail along and pick up the pieces and hope they'll not be bloody."

"You'd faint if they were."

Ryan gave her a wry glance, then laughed. "I would, wouldn't I? I guess I'll just have to keep you safe then."

They rode in a companionable silence the rest of the way to the gray limestone mansion on Ong, a very few blocks but several million dollars from where they lived. Juan of the purple jacket led them into the library, a room with bookshelves for walls, comfortable chairs, a long library table with low-hanging lights over it, and no fireplace. Megan understood the reason for it—all the flammable books—but without a fireplace, the room was only marginally warmer than a morgue.

"Megan, Ryan! Good to see you. Juan, coffee, please. You will have coffee, won't you, Megan?

Megan nodded. A cup full of hot coffee would at least serve as a hand warmer.

Bruce Gorman, casually dressed in expensive khaki slacks and a long-sleeved sports shirt topped by a sweater, sat down at the library table and waved toward the chairs on each side. "Sit down, Megan, Ryan. I presume you have something to report?"

Megan resisted the urge to collapse into one of the many comfortable-looking easy chairs in the room. She still needed to talk Bruce Gorman into one more confrontation with his family, so she had best swallow her tendency toward independent action and take her appointed place at the table. As Ryan pointed out, they were hired help.

Once the purple-coated Juan brought the coffee, and Megan took a sip from a porcelain cup thin enough to see through, it was time to begin the unpleasantness.

"We don't have anything to report, Bruce," said Megan, deliberately using his first name. He might see her as hired help, but that didn't mean she had to act like it. After all, nobody was being paid except Herbert Jackson III, and she would bet that was a pittance. "But I do have two questions that you might be able to answer. First, did Randy pay off Melinda's car when they married?"

"I have no idea what their financial arrangements were, Megan," he said with a slight emphasis on her name, an amused expression in his eyes. Apparently, he recognized her using his first name as a statement of independence.

"Didn't you go through his papers after his death?"

"Paul, his father, took all of his belongings, including any papers or records. I didn't argue. I was in no condition to do so, plus I thought it was Paul's place to take care of his son's estate, particularly since Randy died without a will."

Megan felt her mouth gape open. "Died without a will? How is that possible? Excuse me, Bruce, but you must be able to carpet this house with lawyers."

Bruce Gorman folded his hands and looked away for a moment. Megan saw a slight tremor in his jaw and realized that after twenty years, it still hurt him to talk about Randy. "Of course, he had a will drawn up, Melinda and he both did the day she died, but Randy never made another one, and with Melinda predeceasing him, it was as if he had no will at all because the dead cannot inherit, and neither will allowed for another heir—other than natural issue, which they did not have."

"Who inherited Randy's money and property—if he had any?"

Bruce Gorman looked amused, and Megan wished she hadn't added that codicil to her question. She wasn't used to dealing with the very wealthy—except Ryan who was only very mildly wealthy and didn't live like it. "Randy had a very generous trust fund from his grandfather, as well as a share in Gorman Oil and Gorman Land and Cattle Company. The money and property stayed in the family."

Megan nodded her head and kept her comments to herself. "I have another question to ask you, Bruce, and excuse me, but it's a very personal question. Why did you promote Melinda to the position of your private secretary?"

Bruce Gorman looked startled, then his eyes narrowed and the expression in them would undoubtedly freeze most of his employees. "I don't think I need to defend my managerial decisions. Besides, Melinda's position as my secretary has nothing to do with her death."

"I only have your word for that. Melinda had a lover before she married your grandson. Was it you?"

He tried to stare her down, but Megan had been stared at by experts, like one physical anthropology professor whose stare skewered her when she misidentified a bone—or rather a piece of a bone. "I see why you have been successful at solving crimes, Miss Clark. You don't back down to anybody, do you?"

"I never saw any reason to, and it's damaging to the self-esteem besides. And I'm a short, cute female. Short, cute females either learn to fight or are forever doormats. I'm not a doormat."

"Is she always like this, Ryan? Stubborn and determined?"

"Pretty much. If you try arguing with her, we'll be here the rest of the day."

Bruce Gorman rubbed his chin, then focused on Megan. "I wasn't Melinda's gentleman friend. I would have been, if she had indicated any kind of interest in me. Twenty years ago, I could still please the ladies, but I guess she thought I was too old. She was a beautiful woman and frankly, she was on the make—as we used to call it. At first she played up to all the Gorman men, but my son, Paul, is a cold, virtuous man and doesn't care for flirtatious women. He called her into his office one day—this was before she was my secretary—and what he said to her I don't know, but when she walked out his door, her behavior was much more circumspect. And once she started going out with Randy, she cut out any kidding or teasing. Unlike the rest of the family, I have no objections to young women using their natural assets to better themselves, so long as they keep the bargain once they make it. Melinda was determined to be a good wife to Randy, and I think she would have made him one. Maybe not the junior leaguer kind, but she would have held up her end of our social obligations. She would have kept her bargain."

"Not a very romantic picture of the marriage."

"Randy had enough of the romantic to make up for the rest of us, and it killed him."

Megan looked down at her hands, still folded around her cup, and took another sip to delay the second round of unpleasantness. Ryan might think her tough, and she might present herself as such, but she hated confrontation as much as anyone. She just didn't shy away from it when it was necessary.

"So you made her your secretary because you wanted to, uh, hit on her?" Megan noticed Ryan flinching at her choice of language.

"No, I promoted her because Paul recommended her. I'm a wealthy man because I promote the best. Had Melinda not been competent, Paul wouldn't have recommended her, and I would have sent her back to the typing pool. I don't waste money on the incompetent."

"How long was she your secretary?"

"Only a month or two before Randy graduated and came to work. Once she met him, we all saw what was happening, and frankly I was happy about it. As I said, Melinda was a competent young woman—much like my father's second wife—and I thought the family could use a competent woman. And I was very glad then that she had showed no interest in flirting with me, so I suffered no inner conflict about her marrying Randy. Not that a man is ever too old to be jealous, Megan, but I loved my grandson too much to begrudge him a beautiful woman."

"But someone else did?" asked Megan.

Bruce Gorman drew a sudden breath, as if he had only just remembered to breathe. He lowered his head to stare at his folded hands with the prominent veins and liver spots. When he looked up, Megan barely stopped herself from gasping, so ill and old did he look.

"My son, Paul, told me that I would regret asking you for help because you might provide it. Already you have forced me to face the terrible prospect that the murderer is most likely one of my own family. What began as a search for my own peace of mind has become a search for justice, and I fear that more than I have feared anything in my life. There is a reason why Justice is blind, Megan. It is so she will not be swayed by an old man who only wants to die in peace. As a result of loosing you upon my family, I will most assuredly end my life in regret."

Megan blinked away tears. "Even if you fire me, I won't quit, Mr. Gorman." She felt Ryan reach across the table and clasp her hands.

"I suspected that—and call me Bruce. We're equals, I think, in wishing we had never started this search."

"Do you know which of your family was Melinda's

lover?" asked Megan, swiping her eyes on her sleeve.

Bruce Gorman's eyes grew hard as granite. "If I did, I would have confronted him myself and not exposed my family to ridicule."

"But how would that have served justice, since I doubt you would have turned him over to the police for prosecution?"

"If it were Paul, I would reduce him to poverty, because he has only what he has earned and will inherit. For a man as proud as Paul, that would suffice as much as a death sentence. My grandsons would be more of a challenge as they all have trust funds, but I would deprive them of any part of the Gorman property and pass the word around social circles that I would not be present at any function to which they were also invited. I would say that was nearly as good as the Amish ritual of shunning. Jake would certainly despise such treatment."

"Jake the snake," whispered Megan without conscious thought.

Bruce Gorman nodded. "He's always been an arrogant young pup. But he's not a young pup anymore, and I find his arrogance tiresome." He scooted his chair back and rose. "Would you like to speak to him? He and Trent are here for their usual Saturday afternoon of nagging at Grandfather in hopes I will retire and leave them in charge of the businesses. I mourn Randy's death more on Saturday than any other day of the week, because I had planned to turn over all the Gorman assets to his management. He was a good supervisor of people, certainly better than the rest of us, without being mean about it. He was a good man, and a fair man even though very young, and I miss him more the closer I come to the end myself. What will happen to the Gormans when

I'm gone, Megan? You must find me answers, so I will know what to do."

He walked toward the door, his steps the unsteady ones of an old man. "I'll send in Jake, then Trent. Perhaps you'll learn something from them."

16

"You know enough about me to know that I can't stand losing. Only nice people lose."

ROBERT RYAN
(psychotic millionaire Smith Ohlrig) to Barbara Bel
Geddes (model Leonora Eames),
Caught, 1949

I squeezed Megan's hands. They were as cold as the room, and that was cold enough to chill wine—and I didn't see any afghans to wrap Megan in. "Are you sure you to want to talk to this jerk again? You already know he won't answer any questions, or at least not answer them truthfully."

She looked at me, her face wan, and freed her hands. I didn't take offense. After all, who would believe she was in charge if she held hands with me?

"Maybe I can learn something from his lies," she said.

"That's the problem. How do you tell the difference?"

She didn't say anything, so I poured us another cup of coffee, and we waited. It was a pleasant room; with five or six space heaters, it might even be comfortable. I wondered how Bruce Gorman could have stood living in this mausoleum all his life.

The door opened, and Jake Gorman walked in wearing a blazer over a heavy-knit polo shirt. Smart man.

"Dr. Clark, my grandfather said you had questions you wanted to ask me."

"Did he tell you to answer them?" asked Megan, calmly sipping her coffee and gazing at him over the rim of her cup.

A glitter of resentment appeared momentarily in his eyes, then vanished, but not before I saw it. "He was rather emphatic about it. I don't appreciate his change in personality since meeting you and listening to your nonsense about how Melinda's murderer was a Gorman—a Gorman rather than Randy, that is."

"You believe your cousin murdered his wife?" asked Megan, her expression remote, as though she was observing Jake Gorman as she might a snake in a glass cage: waiting for him to strike, but knowing she was safe from his venom.

"What is my alternative?"

"Actually, none." Megan sat her cup down and clasped her hands together. "Melinda Gorman had a lover before she married Randy. Was it you?"

Jake blinked, and I knew from the brief glimpse of his eyes that he was surprised by her question, maybe even shocked. "I believe I said before that I don't fraternize with the help. She flirted for a while, but then gave it up."

"So you didn't make the cut," said Megan.

Jake Gorman half rose from his chair. "What's that supposed to mean?"

"You were rejected in favor of someone else."

"She was a cheap piece of—"

"Watch it!" I shouted. I was on my feet with clenched fists and leaning over Jake Gorman ready to hammer him into the oak library table. "You can answer questions without using gutter language."

"Excuse me, Professor. I didn't realize Dr. Clark had such delicate ears," said Jake with what might be construed as a sneer on his face. There was no way out as far as I was concerned. I would simply have to beat the tarnation out of Jake the snake before this case was over.

"Sit down please, Ryan," said Megan, reaching out to grasp my arm. "I only have one more question to ask Jake, and then he can slither off to his den. What did you talk to Randy about on the day he committed suicide?"

Again I caught a brief expression of surprise in Jake's eyes. Whatever questions he anticipated, they were not the ones Megan asked. "I told him it was time to put Melinda's murder behind him, that she was dead, and no one could bring her back. I told him that Granddad had announced that Randy would be taking over running the business, and that he needed to get a grip on himself. I told him that Melinda wasn't worth moping over for years. We got in a fight over that, and he chipped my tooth. It cost me a bundle to have it capped."

"When did your grandfather announce that Randy would be taking over the business?"

"The day before, I guess, or a couple days before. I know that Trent and I were mad about it because it was like we were passed over, and both of us were older than Randy."

"What about Paul?" asked Megan. "Wasn't he angry?"

"Paul? Paul has ice instead of blood. You never see him angry, not ever."

"Who was in charge after Randy committed suicide?"

"Paul was. There was some talk of Jimmy taking over when he was older, but you saw him, Dr. Clark. He can barely take care of himself. Once Paul steps down, then

Trent and I will take over. Jimmy can stay on the ranch playing cowboy. It's about all he can do now."

"Did Jimmy overhear your argument?"

"Well, he was standing there, then he took up for Randy by tearing into Trent. Everybody was bleeding by the time Granddad and Paul got upstairs. Granddad sent Trent, Jimmy, and me downstairs, while Paul took Randy to his room to help him wash the blood off. Randy got the worst of it because I was a better fighter. Michele came about then and started screaming. Paul got her into Randy's bedroom, and I guess he tried to calm her down, but I heard the three of them shouting. Granddad threw Trent and me out, told us to go mind our own business, and he would take care of his."

"Who do you think Melinda's lover was?"

Jake smirked. "It must have been Granddad. He had the most money, and Melinda wanted money."

"Do you have any proof of your accusation?" asked Megan, barely holding on to her remote expression. I could see the disgust in her eyes from where I was sitting.

"About as much proof as you have, lady, which is none."

"If your grandfather was Melinda's lover, then do you think that he was her murderer?" asked Megan.

"Why does it have to be the same person?" asked Jake with another smirk.

"Oh, it doesn't," replied Megan, pushing her chair back and rising. "You may go now while I talk to your cousin Trent."

I watched her follow Jake the snake to the door, probably to make sure that he and Trent didn't cook up a story between them. While I was waiting for her to come back escorting Trent for his interrogation, I mulled over

Megan's questions and Jake's answers. What did she mean by insinuating that one person was Melinda's lover, while a different person killed her—unless she was talking about the wives. If Michele Gorman had been contemplating murdering Melinda, it would explain her wild bidding. It would also explain why she calmed down. She had gotten her hatred out of her system by murdering Melinda. The slut was dead.

But that would only work if Paul was Melinda's lover, and Michele was getting her vengeance. But that didn't make sense either, because Bruce Gorman said that once Melinda met Bruce, she stopped all flirting with other men. The same scenario played out if Trent was her lover and Deanne killed Melinda. Why kill her once the affair was over? It might not be pleasant to put up with your husband's ex-lover as a member of the family, but it would surely be safer than murdering her.

Or perhaps Michele killed Melinda so she wouldn't cause trouble between her sons. But if that was the case, why did Randy commit suicide? Did he discover his mother was a murderer? That would surely set him off. But how did he discover she was a murderer? She wasn't likely to admit it, and I doubt anyone else would tell him. No, I think Megan was a little off with the different lover–different killer theory. And Jake was right about one thing: Bruce Gorman had more money that God, so if all Melinda was interested in was money, then old man Gorman was the lover-murderer. And if that was true, it was no wonder he didn't sleep well at night; his conscience was hurting him.

Of course, there was young Jimmy, but he was only a teenager at the time. But teenagers are reservoirs of testosterone. Maybe Jimmy mistook flirting for something more serious. Perhaps he met Melinda in the gazebo and killed her when she wouldn't agree to continue any intimacy. Then, when Randy committed suicide, little Jimmy went bonkers and was sent to the psychiatric ward to deal with his guilt feelings. The problem was, I liked Jimmy, and I didn't like seeing him cast as a murderer. Which is another reason why Megan is the sleuth and I'm Watson. I couldn't pin a murder on someone I liked. Megan has done it before. I don't think she enjoyed it, but she did it just the same.

And while I was on the subject of Jimmy, why didn't he tell us about the fight the day Randy committed suicide? Did he believe the fight had nothing to do with the suicide? Or was the fight one more reason Jimmy cracked up? He couldn't stand to think Jake or Trent pushed Randy over the edge.

Megan walked back into the library, escorting a very sullen Trent, and sullen didn't look good with his face-lift. "Would you like me to call for more coffee, Trent?"

"This is my grandfather's house. Where do you get off ordering the help around?" demanded Trent in a belligerent tone.

There was that word again: *help*. Which reminded me. Megan hadn't asked any questions about the three prematurely dead servants. I wondered why.

"I guess that's a no," said Megan, ignoring Trent's tone. "So let's get down to the questions I have for you, so you and your cousin can go do whatever rich men do on Saturday afternoons.

"Play golf."

"I beg your pardon?" said Megan.

"You asked what rich men do on Saturday afternoons, and I told you: we play golf."

Megan raised her eyebrows. "Now to more important

subjects. Melinda had a lover before she married Randy. Was it you?"

Did you ever see anyone actually fumble for words? Trent Gorman did. He opened his mouth, nothing came out—which made him look like a gaping goldfish—then he stuttered for several seconds before he finally laid hands—or tongue—on the word he wanted. "No!" he shouted. "And I resent the implication of that question."

Megan cut him off before he could go into the said implications at any length. "That's interesting. Jake insinuated it was you.

"What? That bastard!" His face was that fuchsia color again, and my mouth had fallen open.

Megan pursed her lips. "You still maintain that it's not true?"

"If it was anyone, it was Jake! He was sniffing around her like she was a dog in heat."

"Watch the language! We don't need any colorful similes. We need the absolute truth," I warned him while turning a glowering look at Megan that told her she was included. She had the audacity to look innocent.

"So you believe that Jake was her lover?" asked Megan.

Trent was sweating. "I didn't say that! I said he was after her like we all were, and she played up to us, too, even my dad, and he's the coldest fish around. But nobody got to her that I know of, and she cooled off after my father reamed her out one day."

"Then you don't believe that your grandfather was her lover either?" asked Megan.

"My grandfather! He was an old man by that time. I bet he couldn't even get it—" Trent looked at me and swallowed his last word, which was a healthy thing for him to do. I'd had about enough of the Gormans' rough language.

"What did you say to Randy that last day before he committed suicide?"

For the first time, I saw Trent Gorman look his age. His face looked like a smooth mask, but his eyes gave him away. They were old, red-veined, and anguished.

"I told him that Melinda wasn't worth mourning for a year, that she had made up to everybody in the office before he graduated and came to work." He looked up at us, tears glistening in those old eyes. "I was mad at him, so mad I didn't think what I was saying. Granddad had announced the day before that Randy was being put in charge of Gorman Oil, and I wanted a fight. I wanted to hurt him, but I never meant to say anything that sent him over the edge like that. And then we had to put up with the whole town saying he was guilty, and his suicide proved it. And now you're here and stirring it all up again. We won't be able to go to a single social function without people talking behind our backs."

Until he started whining, I had nearly persuaded myself to feel a little sorry for him—not much, but a little.

"Do you feel responsible for Randy's suicide?" asked Megan.

"I think my parents believe I am."

"Then why would Jimmy have a nervous breakdown from guilt if it was your fault?"

Trent shook his head. "I don't know about that. I just know that Jimmy was upstairs when Randy shot himself later that afternoon."

"Excuse me for interrupting, Dr. Clark, but I think we've had enough of your questions."

Paul Gorman stood in the door to the library, his eyes laser beams of disapproval. His black hair barely frosted with gray was coiffed as if he were an anchorman on the news, his khakis pressed, and long-sleeved sports shirt neatly tucked in. He was the man in charge, and he raised my hackles about as badly as anyone ever had. As for Megan, her features settled into her remote mode again, and I knew Paul Gorman wasn't about to budge her.

Megan glanced over her shoulder as if his presence didn't call for more than a glance. "Come in, Paul, I had just finished asking some follow-up questions of Trent, and now I can ask you a couple of things I failed to ask the other evening."

"I don't believe I have any answers for you."

Megan crossed her arms back of her head and stretched, then lowered her arms. "Have you spoken with your father about your reluctance to answer questions, Paul?" she asked without bothering to glance at him.

As a threat, it was effective. Paul Gorman's nostrils flared, and he cast a look of such absolute hate at Megan that I felt chills prickle along by spine. I half rose to protect her, but Paul merely jerked his chin at his son, and Trent left the library at practically a run. Paul quietly closed the door behind his son, and the chills along my spine turned to icicles. There was something so unhumanly controlled about closing that door with barely a sound when the average man would have slammed it shut.

Paul sat down at the head of the table where his father had sat and folded his hands. A calm man in perfect control of his environment. Actually, he matched the environment. One was about as cold as the other.

"What is it you wish to ask me, Dr. Clark?"

"Were you Melinda's lover?"

His nostrils flared again. I wished I could do that. It looked so aristocratic.

"What left field did that come out of, Dr. Clark?" His voice was still a controlled baritone, but one had the feeling he was screaming somewhere inside.

"Melinda had a lover before she met Randy. Was it you?"

"My God, Dr. Clark, I'm a fastidious man, and I didn't know where she'd been!"

Melinda evolved from a plain slut to a diseased one in a single sentence. Paul Gorman was by far the slickest of the family. His only competition so far as I could see was Jake the snake.

"Do you know who it might have been?" Megan asked, her expression still remote, but I noticed her hands were no longer visible, resting on her lap out of Paul Gorman's sight. I suspected they might be trembling from the stress involved in questioning four Gorman men, only one of whom acted in a gentlemanly manner. Even Megan is not invincible.

"If I were guessing, and let me emphasize that it is only a guess, I would name Jake. He is used to taking what he wants."

"What about your father?"

Paul closed his eyes as though he had received an unexpected blow. When he opened them again, the shutters were up. Paul Gorman would not reveal any more information. "That is an obscene suggestion."

"What about Jimmy?"

There was no flinching this time. Apparently Paul Gorman had expected to be questioned about Jimmy. "That is another obscene suggestion, and I plead with you, Dr. Clark, not to put such a suggestion to Jimmy. I don't know what his reaction would be, and I don't want to find out. He is reasonably stable now, and I want him to stay that way. I've already lost a son to suicide; I don't want to lose another to insanity."

"You committed Jimmy after the suicide. What kind of therapy did he receive that he has not yet realized that being angry about Randy's suicide is a normal human reaction?"

"My son's treatment for mental illness is a confidential matter, Dr. Clark, and I will not share it with you."

"What was the psychiatrist treating him for if not his anger?"

"Again, that is none of your business. If you were a private detective, I would institute moves to have your licence to operate revoked. As it is, you're a rank amateur who is interfering with the peace of this family."

Megan shrugged her shoulders. "At the request of your father."

"I really don't care at whose request it is, I intend to stop your snooping."

"A power play against your father?"

Paul Gorman clenched his teeth, and I saw a tiny muscle ripple along his jawline. I don't think he liked being reminded that he was still under his father's thumb. "The dynamics of my family are also none of your business, Dr. Clark."

"I understand from your father that Randy in effect died without a will. How was his money and property divided?"

"His trust fund was divided between his two brothers, Trent and Jimmy. His mother and I inherited the rest."

"What about Melinda's car?"

For the first time, Paul Gorman was caught off guard by one of Megan's questions. His face went slack for a split second before he recovered. "I sold it."

"Was it paid for?"

"My lawyers handled the estate, Dr. Clark. I wouldn't know such minor details."

"But you sold it yourself?"

"Any mention of Melinda Mitchell after my son's suicide would send my wife into a depression. You can imagine the effect on her if I had allowed Melinda's car on our property. I left it in Dad's garage and sold it immediately."

"Then it was paid for, and you had the title?" asked Megan.

Paul Gorman looked impatient. "Apparently I must have had the title, or I couldn't have sold it. I don't remember the exact details, Dr. Clark. It's been twenty years, and I was concerned with disposing of any reminder of Melinda Mitchell as quickly as possible for the sake of my wife's sanity."

"Gorman," said Megan quietly.

"What?" asked Paul Gorman, his brow wrinkling in confusion.

"Her name was Gorman when she died."

17

"If you think I have any qualms about killing this kid, you couldn't be more wrong. The thing about killing him, or you, or her, or him is that I wouldn't be getting paid for it—and I don't like giving anything away for free."

FRANK SINATRA
(contract killer Johnny Baron),
Suddenly, 1954

Megan tied the laces on her hiking boots and stood up. She yawned, stretching her arms as high as she could reach—which wasn't very high when you were barely five feet, two inches, if you wore shoes. She glared at Rembrandt and Horatio Hornbeagle, both pacing around her feet and whining. "I don't know what you two were barking at last night, but you both better put a cork in it tonight, or my mother is liable to gag you and make you spend the night in the garage. No soft beds or couches or easy chairs, just cold, hard concrete. Remember, this is her house, and you two live here on sufferance."

Two beagles grinned at her, long pink tongues hanging out one side of their mouths.

"Yeah, right, that's a big threat, isn't it? Mom's the one who wraps each of you in an afghan if she thinks you might be cold."

The beagles tilted their heads to one side, cocking their long, floppy ears, which Megan always thought made them look like they were wearing Egyptian head-dresses, and listening to her as though she were a god-dess. "All right, Rembrandt, Horatio, let me open the back door, and I'll escort you to the backyard, so you can step in any mud you can find and bark at the poor squirrel that is gathering nuts and minding his own busi-ness. Oh, yeah, and you'll want to exchange insults with the two pugs down the alley. Just remember, they can't help it if they don't have long noses and floppy ears and spots. Not everybody is as beautiful as you two."

Megan unlocked the back door and opened the screen. Instantly, the two beagles ran between her legs toward her truck, parked in the driveway at the back of the house. They both began barking at the truck's hood, with Horatio trying to jump on top, missing, and sliding his nails down the side, leaving narrow scratches.

"Horatio! Stop it! What's wrong with you two? Rem-brandt, shut up. You'll wake the town with your bel-low!"

She caught the two dogs by their collars, dragging them away from her truck. It might be ten years old, have 300,000-plus miles, and look like it had driven through a forest of mesquite—which it had, one summer when she was on a dig—but she didn't want Horatio adding any more scratches.

"Hush, now," she said, trying to quiet them. "What's the matter with the truck? Is there a cat sleeping under the hood? Be quiet now, and I'll look."

She let go of the dogs and peered in the open window of the truck's extended cab. There was the usual clutter in the backseat—ropes, shovel, tire chain—but nothing unusual. She opened the door and popped the hood release, then went around to lift the hood. "I'm going to show you dogs, especially you, Horatio, that there's nothing wrong."

She peered under the hood. "Oh, my God!" she cried, and grabbed both dogs by their collars, dragging them across the yard.

"Ryan! Oh, dear God, Ryan, let me in!" she screamed outside his back door.

Ryan opened the door wearing pajama bottoms, shaving lather on one side of his face, and a confused look. "Megan! What's the matter?"

"There's a bomb in my truck!" she screamed, stumbling into his kitchen, and then into his arms, dragging two barking beagles with her.

Lieutenant Jerry Carr sat on the couch next to Ryan. Wrapped in a blanket, Megan sat on Ryan's lap, sipping some of his best whiskey. Much as she hated looking like a helpless woman, she couldn't bring herself to get off Ryan's lap. She had faced snakes in her tent on a dig in the Yucatan, scorpions in her shoes in Israel, terrorists shooting up the archaeologists's camp in Jordan, but nothing had frightened her more than those two deadly red cylinders of dynamite taped under the hood of her beloved truck. Moreover, she felt violated, defiled. What she didn't feel was mad. She was still too frightened for that. But anger would come. She was certain of it, and when it did, she would mop the floor with this cowardly—she sought for words harsh enough to describe him—*bastard* who lacked the guts to face her. Redheads had a reputation for volatile tempers, and by God, she intended to live up to it. Furthermore, she was short, and that ought to make her twice as tough. But that would all come later. For now, she would sit on

Ryan's lap, cuddled in his arms, sip good whiskey, and recharge her emotional batteries. The realization that someone hated and feared her enough to attempt to blow her to pieces—and she had no doubt that *pieces* was the correct noun—she needed the comfort of a man who was her very best friend, who cared about her—even loved her in a sense—to balance the hatred of her attempted murderer. Only someone who has been a victim of pure hate can appreciate the necessity for restoring the balance between love and hate, that balance the Greeks called the Golden Mean. She smiled at herself. Leave it to an anthropologist/archaeologist, a student of ancient civilizations, to even know such a term as *Golden Mean*. What trivia one thought of after dodging a bomb.

The bomb squad had been there and gone for more than two hours, and Jerry and another cop from Special Crimes, along with Herb Jackson, had been patiently waiting for her to pull herself together to answer questions, but she couldn't stop shaking. Herb had been fluttering around, refilling her whiskey glass, bringing her water, asking if she needed another blanket. If he could cluck, he would be the perfect mother hen. Ryan, still dressed in pajama bottoms, but with an old plaid robe on to preserve his modesty, had wiped off the lather on his face without finishing his shave. Poor Herb, immaculate as usual in his three-piece lawyer suit, winced each time he looked at Ryan's half-shaven face. Ryan himself acted as if he were casually dressed in his professor clothes and lecturing to a classroom full of students. He sent Megan's mother home to call the doctor, make hot soup, and fluff the pillow, despite Megan's protestations that she didn't need to go to bed, but no one was listening to her, and she couldn't blame them. Burrowing your face into Ryan's neck and periodically bursting into tears wasn't much of an illustration of emotional stability.

On the other side of Ryan, as close as they could get to her, sat Rembrandt and Horatio. Periodically, Horatio let loose with a commentary on people and events, but his woof-woof-woof made Jerry Carr wince, and Ryan would absentmindedly pet the beagle to calm him. In fact, Megan heard Ryan talking baby talk to both dogs. She couldn't understand why she hadn't noticed it before, but he was nearly as bad as her mother. And to think she had believed that he didn't really like Rembrandt and Horatio. There's nothing like a near-death experience to make you think more deeply and reexamine your impressions and opinions.

"Megan, are you able to answer some questions now?" asked Jerry Carr. "Maybe you can sit on the couch or that chair. I'm sure the doc could use a rest. His legs are probably going to sleep."

"I'm fine! She's not going anywhere," said Ryan, a twitch under his left eye. Bless his heart, but he did hate being called "the doc."

"I'll just sit h-here," said Megan, trying to control her stutter. She never stuttered, at least, had never stuttered in her life until now. Bombs were definitely injurious to your nerves and vocal cords, even if they didn't explode.

"I believe Dr. Clark had better stay where she is, Lieutenant Carr," said Herb Jackson in that grave voice of his that always reminded Megan of an undertaker making arrangements for a very expensive funeral. "We have to be concerned with shock, you know, and she apparently prefers Professor Stevens's care to anyone else's. Forcing her to move might disturb her emotional equilibrium to the extent that she would require hospitalization—which would, of course, delay your questioning her. Such a course of action would raise questions by the media."

"What media?" demanded Jerry. He motioned to the other cop. "Wilson, go look out the window. There wasn't any press out there a few minutes ago."

Herb continued, "On the other hand, I realize the gravity of the situation and its danger to Dr. Clark, as I'm sure the press does also, and know the sooner you investigate the whereabouts of the various Gormans, the more likely you are to discover the perpetrator of this dastardly act."

Megan put her hand over her mouth to hold in hysterical giggles. Dastardly act? No wonder Herb's work in progress was filled with ancient clichés; so was Herb.

"Lieutenant," said Wilson, trotting back into the room. "The street and yard is teeming with press. We got all the TV stations, the newspaper, the radio stations. Looks like they got every kind of equipment except directional microphones."

Jerry Carr raked his fingers through his hair. "How the devil did they find out so soon? Did the chief call them?"

"My mother did," said Megan.

Jerry sank back on the couch. "Your mother. I forgot about your mother. She handles the media better than a White House press secretary. And why not? She probably has more practice. My God, the chief will blow up when he hears about this."

Megan didn't say anything. Any woman who fought the Department of Energy to a standstill over its plan to dump the nation's nuclear waste in the middle of the Texas Panhandle's most agriculturally productive land could certainly handle Amarillo's chief of police.

"I believe Mrs. Clark's objective was to focus media

attention on her daughter's activities concerning the Gormans. She felt strongly that if the whole town knew what the Gormans were up to, then Dr. Clark would be safe. In fact, it is actually in the interests of the Gormans to protect Dr. Clark so as to avoid bad publicity and its subsequent attention."

"The police can protect Megan Clark!" shouted Jerry.

Herb clucked. "Remember Dr. Clark's nerves, Lieutenant. You may question Dr. Clark as long as your attitude is nonthreatening."

Jerry's face was the color of an old brick. "I'm not going to use a rubber hose on her, Mr. Jackson, and I don't threaten victims of a crime."

"Then you may speak with Dr. Clark, but I will, of course, be present to protect her rights," continued Herb, pulling up the creases in his trousers and taking a seat on an easy chair adjacent to the couch.

"Did you see anyone around your truck, Megan?" asked Jerry, setting a tape recorder on the coffee table after identifying her and himself and giving the date and time. His face was still red, and he had a twitch under his right eye to match Ryan's.

"If I had seen anyone messing with my truck, I would have peppered him with buckshot," said Megan. "That truck went with me from my freshman year in college all the way through my doctoral program. It's a member of my family, and I won't have some sneak trying to blow it up!"

"Megan," said Ryan in a gentle voice. "I don't think that sneak cared as much about blowing up your pickup as he did about blowing up you."

Megan's hands began to shake, and she clasped them tighter around her whiskey glass. "I know it, and I'm mad about it. But I'm no Eva Payne. I know when somebody wants to kill me, and I *won't* be blown up!" She stopped and took a breath. "It's one of the Gormans, Jerry. There's nobody else it could be. I'm getting too close to the Gorman murderer, and he—or she—is trying to stop me."

"He doesn't have to stop you; I will," said Jerry. "Your sleuthing days are over, Megan. In fact, your whole little circle of friends can retire from the investigating business. It's time to let the professionals take over."

"You've been in charge for twenty years, and what have you done? Nothing. You didn't uncover Melinda Gorman's lover, you didn't even know about him."

"What about the lover? Who is it, and how did you find out?"

Megan evaded his eyes. "I don't know who it is, but I know there was one."

"Now there's something I can take to the DA. How do you know there's a lover?"

"Logic."

Jerry Carr got up and paced the room. Megan thought the exercise might be good for him if it relieved some of his stress. His face was still that unhealthy red color.

He whirled around to face her. "Logic! Did you say logic? It would have been logical to tell Bruce Gorman to peddle his papers elsewhere. It would have been logical to come to me with whatever proof you had of a lover. It would have been logical for you and your nutty friends to talk about the Gorman case up one side and down the other, but not to play amateur sleuth. Damn it, Megan! You're not a character in some storybook!"

"At least you didn't call me Nancy Drew," she said. She noticed her hands had stopped shaking and she was feeling warmer.

"There are similarities!" Jerry snapped.

"Don't worry, Jerry, she won't go sleuthing again. I'll see to it," said Ryan.

Megan reared back and looked at him. "I beg your pardon?"

Ryan wrapped the blanket more tightly around her until she felt strangled. "If you don't stop pushing, Megan, you're going to be the next victim. You're alive only because that little dog of yours—"

"Horatio Hornbeagle."

"Yes, well, if Horatio hadn't thrown such a fit, you never would have lifted the hood, and I'd be crying over whatever pieces of you could be found. Damn it, honey, you're going to quit this business now!"

Megan heard the endearment and looked at him in astonishment. If she didn't know better, she would think that he was ordering her about and wrapping her up so tightly and calling her honey because he—well, he loved her. But that was impossible, because he was her best friend's father.

She looked at Jerry Carr, who was glaring at Ryan. What had poor Ryan done to set off Jerry like that? Well, it didn't matter, because neither of them understood. "Ryan, Jerry, don't you understand that I can't quit? I know something, and the murderer can't let me live, even though I can't figure out what it is I know!"

18

"You're pretty good—but first comes you, second comes you, third comes you, and then comes you. You think you can get away with murder, and I bet you often do."

JOAN BENNETT
(secretary Evelyn Nash) to Paul Henreid (con man John Muller/Dr. Bartok),
Hollow Triumph, 1948

I could have lost her. If her dog hadn't barked, if she hadn't been a woman with a tender heart who would check under her hood for a sleeping cat, if she hadn't recognized the dynamite (all right, I know it's hard to misidentify dynamite, but it's possible), my Megan or what was left of her would have been in the morgue. I survived the death of my wife, but I don't know if I would survive losing Megan. Perhaps it's my age, that time of life when men know they seek out love for the last time, or the fact that my family is grown and have lives of their own, or perhaps my feelings for her are deeper than even I realized, but if Megan, like Eva Payne, had died in an explosion, I don't know how I would have gone on living. She is my best friend, a playmate with whom I share adventures, my intellectual companion, and I dream of her being my lover while recognizing that might never come to pass, so my heart is involved in several different ways. My wife was my helpmate, the mother of my children, my lover, a calm, mature woman without Megan's intensity, sweetness, or her feisty nature. My wife and I would have lived out our lives content with who we were, and I would have admired Megan as a charming girl and my daughter's best friend without falling in love with her. And I might be lying to myself, too, because I was already a widower for a year when Megan came home, so I never had to pass the test of fidelity.

God does allow us some breaks in life.

But because I love her, I try to protect her. It's instinctual in the male mammal. I'm seldom successful in that endeavor, but I do try. I was trying my utmost when I drove her to Sixth Street that night to the Time and Again Bookstore and a meeting of Murder by the Yard Reading Circle. At first I argued about her going. Well, that argument went nowhere, as arguments with Megan often do. She announced her intention of biking to Sixth Street if I wouldn't take her, and she could escape the media still camped on her front yard. I capitulated—as I usually do—because I wasn't going to have her bike all the way to Sixth Street at night. That was asking for one of those useless Gormans to make another attempt at killing her, or some sleaze to mug her. Of course, the Gormans couldn't move out of their homes any more than Megan could without attracting a caravan of media. I didn't know Amarillo had so many media. The newspaper, TV, and radio must have temporarily hired every journalism and communication major at Amarillo College and West Texas A&M, because some of the media camped on my front yard looked hardly old enough to have passed puberty. I wondered their mothers let them stay out past bedtime. And bedtime it was, since Megan's mother said calling a press conference after dark would allow me to back out of my garage with Megan in the floorboard covered by a dark blanket topped by a variety of discarded fast-food sacks and containers left on my yard by the baby journalists. My pickup cab smelled of Big Macs and KFC.

I backed out just as Megan's mom walked out on her front porch and began a press conference, which included both beagles. Once the baby journalists saw the dogs, they paid no more attention to a middle-aged history professor wearing a bow tie made of Christmas ribbon. Dogs were a sure attention getter; bow tie wearers weren't. Once we were a few blocks away, I grabbed for the tie.

"Leave it alone," hissed Megan. "If a stray journalist happens to pass us, he'll ignore you. Who wants to look at somebody wearing a bow tie and with his hair parted in the middle and greased down?"

"Speaking of grease, what in the devil did you put on my hair?"

"I couldn't find any mousse, so I used canola oil."

"What?" I yelled, swerving my truck into the wrong lane before I caught myself. "I'll never get the oil out. I'll go to class looking like Rudolf Valentino."

"Just use some dishwashing detergent."

"My hair will probably fall out."

"Then you'll look like Sean Connery."

"Sean Connery is past sixty!"

"He's still cute. I certainly wouldn't kick him out of bed for eating crackers. And you're obsessing on age again, Ryan."

"Didn't you listen to the news on TV tonight? Didn't you hear that kid call me Nancy Drew's aging Lothario?"

He heard a muffled giggle. "I don't like the Nancy Drew part, of course, but I'm impressed that he knew who Lothario is. That name isn't part of the average person's everyday vocabulary."

"I'm not a seducer!"

"I know it, Ryan, but not everybody understands our relationship."

"Sometimes I don't understand it myself."

The silence from under the blanket drew out until my heart ached before a quiet voice said, "Sometimes I don't either, Ryan."

We left it that way until I drove up the alley by Time and Again Bookstore and parked my truck in the little space behind Agnes's apartment. I turned off the lights, and Megan crept out of the truck and brushed herself off. She knocked at the bookstore's back door, which was also the entrance to Agnes's apartment.

Instantly, a voice asked, "Who goes there?"

"Sherlock Holmes," Megan answered, then elbowed me.

"Watson," I said with a snarl in my voice. I never liked secret passwords.

The back door opened onto darkness. "Come in," said Agnes. "I'll lead you up front by flashlight."

We followed her to the front of the bookstore, where the couch had been left vacant for Megan and me. The other members of the reading circle were seated in the folding chairs pushed as close to the couch as possible. The room was lit by only the light over Agnes's cashier's desk and several vanilla- and magnolia-scented candles on a small table in front of the couch, so our faces weren't in shadow, but the rest of the bookstore was. It was a nice setting for a séance. A thick blanket was taped over the bookstore's one window, so no light fil-

tered out on Sixth Street. The room felt both eerie and
cozy, with wavering light from the candles and huge
shadows cast across the floor by the rows of bookshelves. Faintly, I heard live music from the blues café
down the street, which was appropriate background music for a meeting that felt as if it was lifted straight out
of a film noir. In the place of a butler or a uniformed
maid, Rosemary and Lorene brought Megan and me a
plate of cookies—oatmeal raisin this meeting—and
steaming cups of coffee.

"How's the aging Lothario tonight?"

You might know that Randal Anderson would watch
that particular TV station.

"Love your bow tie," Randal continued.

I looked around for a place to set my cookies and
coffee so I could punch Randal's lights out, but I didn't
get a chance because Candi Hobbs elbowed him in the
tummy—er, belly.

"Be quiet, Randal," she said. "Megan has something
to tell us, and then she has to get back home before the
media know she's gone."

"I saw you on television, Megan, and felt so sorry for
you. Those reporters can be tacky sometimes. And such
personal questions about you and Ryan. It was just terrible," said Rosemary, her face expressing disapproval.

"I liked the way you said it was your investigation
into Melinda Gorman's murder that nearly got you
killed, not your relationship with Ryan. That was putting
those reporters in their place," said Lorene Getz, nod-
ding her white head.

"You had better go ahead and tell us what you have
planned," said Agnes.

I whipped my head around to stare at Megan. Megan
with a plan is dangerous. Megan with a plan could have

ended the Cold War several years before the Berlin Wall came down. Megan with a plan could have frightened Saddam into withdrawing from Kuwait without a fight. In other words, Megan was about to lead me into another predicament.

Megan sipped her coffee, then set her cup down. She was still pale—that is, paler than usual, since she has a peaches-and-cream complexion anyway. She cleared her throat. "I called Bruce Gorman today, and he agreed to host a dinner party tomorrow night, a dinner party with exactly the same guests as were present twenty years ago. Ryan and I will play Randy and Melinda Gorman. Everyone else will play themselves."

"What!" I yelped. "When did you do this? Does Lieutenant Carr know about this? Damn it, Megan, what does it take to persuade you to stay away from the Gormans? A bullet hole between the eyes?"

Megan flinched and turned a little paler, so naturally I felt like a jerk. "I called Bruce Gorman while you were in the shower. I also called Janice and Tommy Mitchell, and they agreed to come. They both have spent a lot of time thinking about that evening and remembering the sequence of events. That should help us re-create the evening as it unfolded. In the meantime, let me tell the rest of you what we've found out."

She recounted our various interviews pretty much word for word: Janice and Tommy Mitchell, the Gormans, the bridge game, Michele's crazy bidding, Tommy Mitchell's Mickey Finn, the shrimp butter sandwiches, Melinda's car.

"It reminds me so much of Agatha Christie's *Cards on the Table*," said Rosemary. "You remember that one, Lorene, where the mysterious host, Mr. Shaitana, invites Superintendent Battle of Scotland Yard, Mrs. Ariadne

Oliver, the mystery writer, Colonel Race of His Majesty's Secret Service, and our own wonderful Mr. Hercule Poirot to a bridge party with four murderers. Of course, Hercule Poirot read clues from the scorecard, just like Megan did."

"And there was no real evidence," added Lorene. "It was all psychological."

"Just like the Gorman case," said Agnes Caldwell, owner of Time and Again Bookstore, and a very sharp woman, in my opinion. As usual, she had put her finger squarely on the problem.

"That's the problem," I said, breaking into the nostalgic discussion of the similarities between Megan Clark and Hercule Poirot—as if Poirot was a real person. "There's no real evidence, Megan. All you have is conjecture, and it's already nearly killed you once. You can't prove a crime entirely by psychology. You prove a crime by using hard science: blood and bullets and fingerprints, and that's Jerry Carr's business."

"That's the whole point, old boy," said Randal. "If Rosemary will forgive me for trespassing on her expertise, let me quote from memory a line from Agatha Christie's foreword to *Cards on the Table*: "The deduction must, therefore, be entirely psychological, but it is none the less interesting for that, because when all is said and done it is the mind of the murderer that is of supreme interest." In other words, Doc, Megan is following in the footsteps of Hercule Poirot by proving a crime by psychology. Who has the psyche most likely to have murdered Melinda? That's what the Gorman case is all about, not fingerprints and blood types."

I *hate* being called Doc. "You can't take that kind of case to a jury."

"We're not the police. We don't arrest somebody and

file charges on him with the DA," said Randal. "All we do is solve the crime and present our reasoning to Bruce Gorman. Let him punish the guilty. From what Megan said, he's got the power of the signature on the will."

"And I know who the guilty person is," announced Megan.

That brought the conversation to a halt—at least, until everyone assimilated what Megan had said. Then there were more questions than at the press conference Megan's mom had called that afternoon. Curiosity in that room reached astronomical heights. Me, I was terrified.

I got up, more determined than I've ever been in my life. "Then I'm calling Jerry Carr. Let him take over."

She grabbed my hand and pulled me back down. For a woman who had spent most of the morning in my lap shaking with terror, she had a steely gaze and a grip a pro wrestler would be proud of. "You still don't understand, Ryan. Somewhere during my investigation, I learned all the information I needed to solve the crime, but I don't know what that information is. In other words, I can prove this case psychologically, but I haven't sorted the facts that support a conclusion. I know the truth, but I don't know it."

"What will you do, Megan?" asked Candi Hobbs.

"She'll call Jerry Carr," I said with as much force as I could muster.

Megan took the time to bless me with a glance that would shrivel wet grass. "I talked to Jerry Carr this morning, and he wasn't impressed, Ryan. Why should I talk to him again?" "Because he carries a gun and can plug anybody who looks cross-eyed at you." I glanced around at the reading circle. Agnes was shaking her head, while Rosemary and Lorene had expressions of pity on their faces. Candi's face was intense, but then she was a graduate student. They turned in their sense of humor when they paid their tuition. Herb looked puzzled, but Herb generally did. Randal had such a smirk on his face that I wanted to hit him.

"What is it? What did I say?" I asked.

Megan covered her face with her hands. "You've got to stop watching those old film noirs on TV, Ryan."

"What? What?"

Megan straightened up and patted my hand. "Never mind, Ryan." She looked around the circle. "As I see it, there is one important question, which I believe is the reason someone went to the risk of making me a car bomb, and it is a question the police never asked: Why did Randy Gorman commit suicide? Because he still grieved and couldn't stand to be under suspicion anymore? But he had stood it for a year. Most grief counselors say that the grieving period lasts a year, then the bereaved are better. Was it the suspicion? But if he was innocent, why commit suicide? If he was guilty, why wait a year? What did Randy Gorman find out that made life so horrible that death was better? What did he find out about his wife's murder that he couldn't live with? What happened on the last day of Randy Gorman's life that drove him to suicide? When I can answer that question, I'll know the murderer's name."

"And you already have the information necessary to answer that question," said Agnes.

"Yes, I believe I do. That's what makes me so dangerous to the murderer."

She stopped and clasped her hands together—I suspect to keep them from shaking. "Shakespeare wrote a play in which his character solved his case by psychology and advice from a ghost, but he couldn't bring his father's murderer to justice without evidence, or a confession, so what Hamlet did was stage a play of his father's murder."

"And look what the hell happened to Hamlet!" I shouted, jumping off the couch to confront the reading circle from a psychologically advantageous height. Not that anybody was impressed.

Megan went on talking as if I wasn't present. "I'll write the dramatic scenario for the reenactment. The only difference between this reenactment and the others we've done on our mystery tour is that the main characters play themselves. Herb, you, Candi, and Lorene play the butler, the maid, and the cook. Rosemary, watch the bridge game and insist the players leave at the same times as they did twenty years ago. Agnes, watch the pool game. Randal, you'll cancel your attendance at the last minute, but you'll sneak into the Gorman yard and hide behind the gazebo, but near enough to its entrance that you can see the murderer approaching."

"Hold it! Hold it right there!" I shouted. "Megan, you're not going to sit out in that gazebo to wait for a murderer! I'll throw my arms around your waist and refuse to let go! I'll tackle you, throw you over my shoulder, tie you up, and lock you in my grandmother's old trunk, but I'll be double damned if I'll let you risk your life!"

I shut up and wiped my sweating forehead on my shirtsleeve. I was sweating all over, icy cold droplets that rolled down my spine, my ribs, and off my forehead to sting my eyes. Imagine the audacity of her trusting Randal Anderson to protect her. Randal Anderson, for God's sake! Well, I wasn't having it. No way, Jose, would I trust Randal Anderson to protect himself, much less Megan. I had made my case, and I meant every word of it. Whatever I had to do to make sure that Megan continued to live in the world, even if I didn't, was what I would do, and the devil with the consequences.

Megan stood up, took my hands in hers, and placed them on her cheeks. Did I ever mention that she had eyes the color of a good Kentucky bourbon: a clear light brown that you lost yourself in?

"Ryan, do you want me to die?" she asked. "Because I will, if we don't go through this enactment. My mother thinks all the publicity will save me, but it won't. Sooner or later, the murderer will come after me. Remember the three servants murdered and the three witnesses gone. I'll be gone, too, buried in some unmarked grave on the prairie in the middle of one hundred and ten sections of Gorman land. We have to unmask him tomorrow night, or I'll never be safe any more than Eva Payne was safe from her husband." Her voice trailed off as she stood quietly in front of me, staring over my shoulder into the dark corners of the bookstore. "Of course, I understand now. Don't worry, Ryan, I'll be safe."

I was motionless also, cupping her face in my hands, watching her, wanting her, knowing she was right about everything except Randal as a bodyguard, and scared literally speechless. "All right," I said finally, my voice trembling.

Randal stood up and clasped my shoulder. "Don't worry, old boy, I'll protect her with my life and a base-ball bat."

I nodded, but I had another idea—an idea I planned to put into play without telling anyone. Megan was my girl, and I intended to protect her as best I could. Fortunately, I had a secret weapon.

19

"Other places are like kindergarten compared to this. It smells so incredibly evil. I didn't think such a place existed except in my own imagination—like a half-remembered dream. Anything could happen here, at any moment."

GENE TIERNEY
(gambler Poppy),
The Shanghai Gesture, 1941

Megan was cold inside and out. The yellow dress with the long sleeves and slim skirt was the best she could do to replicate Melinda's dress of twenty years ago. Had someone told her it was a sundress Melinda wore? She couldn't remember, but surely not. Not in this mausoleum. Her teeth would have been chattering before the first course of dinner was served.

Megan took a deep breath and reached out for Ryan's hand. "Are you ready for the production to begin?"

"No, but I suppose it's too late to talk you out of it."

Holding hands, they walked into the living room or whatever it was called, the room where she and Ryan and Herb first met the Gorman offspring. Smiling, she dropped Ryan's hand and walked toward Janice and Tommy Mitchell, an uncomfortable-looking twosome standing by the fireplace.

"Mother," Megan said, reaching to hug Janice.

The woman stepped back. "Melinda hugged her in-laws before she spoke to us." Janice Mitchell frowned as if it had just occurred to her that her daughter had shown preference for her husband's family over her own. Megan wasn't surprised at Melinda's actions. She was a woman in transition, abandoning one place for another.

Megan patted Janice Mitchell's arm, even if it hadn't happened that way, and wondered how history might have been different if Melinda had not been so anxious to force herself into a place where she was not wanted, because this whole case sprang from that one fact: Melinda was out of place in the Gorman world, and she possessed no skills that would allow her to survive in this rarefied environment. Her needs first drove her into a sexual liaison, then further drove her into a doomed marriage. She met her lover in the gazebo to tell him that she was a married woman and that their relationship was at an end as she attempted to keep her bargain as Randy's wife. Insanely jealous, her lover hit her with a pool cue and strangled her, unaware that Randy's fingerprints were on the pool cue, although Megan doubted it would have made any difference had he known.

Shaking off her thoughts, she led Ryan toward Paul and Michele Gorman. "Michele," she cried, leaning toward the older woman to embrace her.

Michele was board stiff as she endured Megan's hug. "I hope you're happy, Miss Clark, making us play charades."

"I doubt that's what you said to Melinda," said Megan.

"I said nothing to her."

"No, you told her not to touch you," said Deanne. "I

remember, because Paul told you that you owed it to Randy to welcome his wife."

Michele whirled on Deanne. "Shut up!"

Paul Gorman put his hand on his wife's shoulder. "Deanne is right, Michele. That is what you said. We have to be accurate."

Michele looked wildly at her husband, then back at Megan. "Leave us alone."

Paul put his arm around his wife. "Excuse, Dr. Clark, but I need to tend to my wife. I warned my father that this reenactment would be too much for her, but he insisted." He led Michele out of the room.

Megan turned to Deanne. "What did you say to her?"

Deanne looked nervously over her shoulder at her husband. "I said hello. That was all."

"Should I hug Trent? Is that what Melinda did?"

Deanne bit her lip. "No, she didn't hug Trent, only me, and I didn't want her to. Paul hugged her though, but I don't think she wanted him to. I think she was scared of Michele."

Megan glanced over her shoulder toward Jake the snake, curled up on the couch next to the fireplace like the cold-blooded animal he was. If Melinda hugged Jake, Megan didn't intend to carry historical accuracy that far. "What about Jake? How did Melinda greet him?"

"She didn't," said Deanne. "I don't think she liked him much. She didn't exactly ignore Jake, just smiled and walked past him to Jimmy."

"Sounds good to me," said Megan. "Come on, Ryan, let's circle around the snake."

Jimmy sat in the same chair he had when Megan first met him. He was dressed the same way, too, so he was the only one who looked in costume from twenty years in the past. Megan sat down in the chair next to him.

"That's not what Melinda did," he said in that same low voice that couldn't be heard by anyone but her and Ryan.

"What did she do, Jimmy?"

"She kissed me," he said, touching his cheek. "And I lifted her up and whirled her around. It was the only time she and Randy laughed. She had a pretty laugh. But my dad and mom stared holes through me, so I put her down and walked away." He turned his head to stare out the window toward the white, lacy gazebo in the corner of the yard. "I wish I hadn't done that, 'cause I didn't have another chance to hear her laugh."

Megan looked down at the floor to give him a chance to conquer the quiver in his voice, then she asked him the last question to which she had as yet no answer. Once she did, the last piece of the jigsaw puzzle that was the Gorman case would fit neatly into place, and she would be sure she was right.

"Jimmy, when you had your nervous breakdown, what did you tell your therapist was bothering you so much you had to be committed?"

Jimmy rubbed his hands together and looked at her with the expression of a conflicted child. "My dad and mom. They were on Randy's case the day he shot himself, and so were Trent and Jake. Nobody could stand it that Granddad had given Randy control of everything."

"So you weren't committed because Randy killed himself?" asked Megan.

"I felt bad about it because I felt so angry when he did it, and I still feel bad about being angry, but that wasn't what drove me crazy. I was scared then, and I'm still scared now. That's why I stay out on the ranch. I feel safe there. Nobody wants the ranch, just the gas and oil under it."

"Who are you so scared of, Jimmy?" Megan asked, then nodded her head when he answered. The last piece was in place.

"My God, Megan," breathed Ryan.

"It's just like Lieutenant Roberts said. Evil sucks the warmth out of the air, and that's why this house is so cold. Tell Bruce Gorman to serve dinner. Then my dramatic scenario begins."

Megan sat in the gazebo, her stomach queasy, whether from the rich food or from nerves, she didn't know. She hadn't been poisoned, she knew that, because she had not eaten anything that the Gormans didn't eat first. No bad green beans for her. So it must be nerves. It wouldn't be the first time that she had faced a murderer, but it was the first time she'd faced one so evil and in such a beautiful place. A grove of giant cottonwood trees surrounded the lacy, white structure with the onion-shaped dome on its roof. She listened to the melodic sound of the breeze rustling through the cottonwoods and decided they were the only kind of tree in the entire world that truly sang. If it weren't for the fact that she was waiting for a visit from a stone-cold killer, she would curl up on the soft, yellow cushions on the bench that circled the inside of the gazebo, and fall asleep listening to the cottonwood trees singing.

She shifted on the bench in the gazebo, undoubtedly the same place where Melinda sat waiting for her discarded lover, and wondered about the young woman whose dreams died with her. Megan couldn't bring herself to wholly condemn Melinda's actions. Lifting oneself from one economic level to the next is a worthy enough goal, but even twenty years ago, a woman had options other than marrying wealth. But, she reminded herself, Melinda was a girl with many needs who only knew one way to satisfy them. In Melinda's place, Megan knew she would have picked other options, but she recognized that her intelligence and ambition were probably greater. Megan could think of no circumstances under which she would raise herself in the world by riding on a man's coattails, but she understood Melinda's choosing to do so. A woman made use of her assets whatever they were, and in Melinda's case it was physical beauty. And Megan believed with Bruce Gorman that Melinda was prepared to keep her bargain as Randy's wife. That spoke of a kind of honor.

A sound of cries came from the Gorman mansion, and Megan drew a deep breath. "Randal, are you ready? Candi has handed out my notes to our principals, and I expect a visitor very soon."

"I'm sitting on a branch in the cottonwood closest to the gazebo, Megan. What the devil did you write in those notes Candi passed out? It sounds like World War III in the house."

"Oh, I just told each one what their relatives had told me. I expect the resulting arguments will clear out a lot of surplus bile. A family is usually dysfunctional because its members stab one another in the back. I just gave the Gorman family the means to fight one another face-to-face. Except for Jimmy."

"What kind of note did you give to him?" asked Randal.

"I told him he didn't need to be afraid anymore, that the guilty would be punished."

"You two be quiet. Voices carry farther at night than you think."

Megan twisted around on the bench to stare out the side of the gazebo. "Lieutenant Roberts?"

"Yeah, it's me. Ryan figured he needed a secret weapon to protect you. I don't know how secret my weapon is, but I'm packing. Nothing against your baseball bat, son—in certain kinds of fights, you'd do right well with it—but we don't know just how this yahoo is planning to kill Megan. I figure a .357 ought to cut him down to size."

"Thank you, Lieutenant Roberts, but don't do anything until he confesses. I think three witnesses to his confession ought to be enough to convict him. Don't you think, Lieutenant Roberts?"

"What if he just goes right to his business without talking?" asked Roberts.

"He won't. He has too much ego."

"Can it, you two," warned Randal. "Here comes our boy."

Megan felt her heart start to drum in her chest and her hands begin to sweat. She wiped her hands on her skirt as a shadowy figure loomed in the doorway. She swallowed and wished she hadn't chosen to remain true to historical accuracy, because she was meeting a murderer in a tiny building with only one door, and Paul Gorman was blocking it, Paul Gorman and his pool cue.

"I got your note, Dr. Clark. Not a very literate note, but to the point, I suppose."

"I thought writing 'You're it' was all that was necessary."

"You were stupid with your little play and your notes. Thanks to those notes, your hero, Professor Ryan, is trying to separate Jake and my father, so I'm afraid he won't be able to come rescue you. And that anal-retentive lawyer you brought with you is trying to keep my wife and Deanne apart, he and two of your old ladies. But you'd need more than help from two old ladies, now.

"My old ladies are different from most," said Megan. "I believe Rosemary and Lorene take karate classes together. They could give you quite a fight."

"I suspect you think you can give me a fight, too," said Paul, now moving into the gazebo.

Megan scooted away, then got up and began circling the interior of the gazebo, always facing him. He wasn't the kind of man to turn your back on. "You could put down that pool cue so we could have a more equal fight."

"But I like the historical accuracy. Isn't that what you wanted? Historical accuracy? At least, that's what you told my father. I'm just obliging you," said Paul, turning with Megan, but always staying between her and the gazebo's entrance.

"Why did you kill her?" asked Megan. "Why couldn't you let her go?"

"Because she was mine first. I didn't intend to let my son have her."

"And you couldn't kill your son, so you killed her?" asked Megan, knowing the answer already.

"He was, despite his stupidity for marrying into the lower classes, my son."

His slight emphasis on the word *my* sent chills down Megan's back. "You didn't spare him because you loved him but because he was a possession—in a manner of speaking."

"Something like that."

"And the help not being family, and the other three witnesses being strangers, all were expendable."

"Of course."

"Then your father turned over control of the Gorman properties to Randy," said Megan.

"And he became an obstacle."

Megan's queasiness grew. This man saw his own son as an obstacle to be removed. She had known that, but hearing him say it was almost more than she could stomach. "You told him you were Melinda's lover that afternoon before he committed suicide, didn't you?" asked Megan.

"Actually, my dear wife took care of that part of the program; otherwise, I would have been forced to reveal that detail myself. But inadvertently, Michele told Randy that Melinda was nothing but a slut who was sleeping with his father. I don't think Randy had a clue until that point that he and I shared his wife. Michele has been somewhat unstable ever since."

"That's why you told her at our first meeting to be quiet and not to think about it anymore, that it was in the past, that it had happened more than twenty years ago. You were afraid she was going to blurt out that you had been Melinda's lover."

"I saw you frown when I told her that. That was the first moment that I worried you would be able to put it all together. I had, of course, nagged at the police about Melinda's having a lover, but because I was the one insisting, no one thought that I might be using reverse psychology. I am curious about how you figured it out."

"Several things, but the most important question was asking myself who had the most to gain from Randy's suicide. Most domestic murders are committed for lust or money. This case had both."

"Such a simple question. I wonder why the police never thought to ask it."

"I'm sure they did ask it. All the Gormans were sus-

pects, but there was no proof. The police like physical
evidence. I wonder what Lieutenant Roberts's attitude
would have been if he had thought of Randy's murder
as a murder by proxy."

"You're very clever, Dr. Clark. Under different circumstances, I would have enjoyed knowing you better.
We would have made quite a couple," said Paul, moving
closer, holding the cue stick like a bludgeon.

"I don't think so," said Megan, feeling perspiration
trickle down her ribs as she circled away from Paul. "I
like my men warm."

"Like your besotted professor?"

"Yes, like Ryan," she said, and ducked as he swung
the pool cue at her.

"Drop the stick, you damn bastard, or I'll blow your
head off!" shouted Lieutenant Roberts, standing in the
gazebo door behind Paul Gorman with his .357 pointed
at Gorman's head.

Suddenly, Paul dropped the pool cue and fell to his
knees. "Oh, my God, you're here!" he screamed, staring
over Megan's shoulder and cowering away. Then he
grabbed his head and stiffened, falling over on his side.

Megan swallowed and stared into Lieutenant Roberts's eyes. No way was she going to turn around to see
whatever—or whoever—struck Paul Gorman dead.

"Do you see anything?"

Lieutenant Roberts swallowed and stared back into
her eyes. Megan could see the beads of sweat on his
forehead shining in the moonlight. "I ain't looking
'cause I don't want to see nothing."

EPILOGUE

"Dearest Stephanie—if this letter is found on me, if this ever reaches you, I want you to believe every word of it and try to understand. It all began that night we arrived in Istanbul."

VOICE-OVER, JOSEPH COTTON
(armament engineer Howard Graham) to his wife,
Journey Into Fear, 1943

Megan and I sat on the couch again, she because it was the place of honor, and I because I didn't intend to be any more that a few inches away from her. Rosemary and Lorene had brought us a plate of cookies—toll house on this occasion—and steaming cups of coffee. The candles were lit—peach and strawberry were this week's scents—but all of the bookstore's lights were on, so the room was bright, as it should have been for the revealing of Megan's reasoning that led her to accuse Paul Gorman. Shadows are for devious planning; light is for revelation.

"I believe we're ready, Megan," said Agnes, looking attractive in a peach-colored blazer over charcoal trousers. I'd never seen her so feathered out—a cowboy term for dressed up—but then I noticed that she was sitting by Lieutenant Roberts, who is still a fine-looking man at seventy plus. I silently wished Agnes luck. Something good ought to come out of this case.

Leaning over, Megan spoke to the wizened figure sitting in the armchair next to the couch. "Are you certain you want to stay, Bruce? I will be saying some hard things about your family. You may not want to listen."

Looking every year of the eighty-six he claimed, plus several more, Bruce Gorman patted her hand and shook his head. "I asked you and this reading circle to learn who murdered Melinda and why my grandson committed suicide. You uncovered the man responsible. Now I want to know what clues you found that Lieutenant Roberts missed in his investigation, and what personality traits Paul had that I never noticed. It's a terrible thing at my age to realize you fathered a monster and didn't have the good sense to see it. My son murdered eight people. I owe it to society and to what remains of my family to hear the story. I don't want to, but I must."

Megan nodded, then scooted to the front of the couch and gazed around at the circle. I watched her for any sign of post-traumatic stress syndrome. Isn't that what the doctors call a sudden reaction to some past traumatic event? Megan had fallen into my arms after her confrontation with Paul Gorman and his sudden death, but there was always the chance she might have a relapse, and I wanted to be close if she did. I'll take any excuse to offer comfort to Megan, particularly if it means I can hold her in my arms. If that makes me a bad person, I can live with it.

"I thought this case was about who murdered Melinda Gorman," began Megan, "but I was only half right. The case was also about why Randy Gorman committed suicide. Until I realized that, I was just as uncertain about the identity of the murderer as Lieutenant Roberts was the day he retired from the police department. In fact, it was asking myself why Randy would commit suicide that pointed out the solution—that and our mystery tour."

"What could the mystery tour have to do with the Gorman case?" asked Randal, preening like some bedraggled rooster. Randal had been a pain ever since he had stood guard with Roberts. I don't know why he should think so highly of himself when it was Roberts who drew down on Gorman. *Drew down* is another term you run across in western novels.

Megan nibbled on a cookie and took a sip of coffee while suspense built. Just when we were all ready to shake her, she began her story. She has a terrific sense of timing.

"Each one of our old murder cases has something in common with the Gorman case. I first noticed it when I interviewed Jimmy Gorman. He's thirty-six years old, but he seems more the boy he was twenty years ago. It was as if he stopped maturing and aging when Melinda died. He was still a frightened boy—just like Sheriff James Gobel was frightened—and for the same reason. Someone that Jimmy—and Sheriff Gobel—thought he could trust might possibly harm him, even kill him. The knowledge devastated both of them. Sheriff Gobel reacted by defending himself and shooting the man he believed was ordered to kill him. Jimmy reacted by having a nervous breakdown because he *couldn't* defend himself. He would have to kill his own father, and he chose mental illness over that. But not until last night, when I asked him who he feared, was I entirely sure that Paul was the murderer."

"What did he say?" asked Lorene Getz, who, now that I looked at her, was also gussied up. Lieutenant Roberts was liable to find himself the center of more attention than he wanted or needed.

"Jimmy said he felt safe on the ranch because no one wanted it, just the gas and oil under it, and that he feared his father. By managing the ranch, Jimmy was not a threat to his father."

Megan took another sip of coffee. "Now comes the Tex Thornton case, a case about sex and money and a woman—girl really—who was willing to trade one for the other. Melinda was not the manipulative, promiscuous girl that Diana Heaney Johnson apparently was, but she also traded sex for a step up on the economic ladder. Like Lena Sneed, she felt trapped and tried to free herself as best she could. But her husband couldn't kill her lover, as Diana Johnson claimed Evald Johnson killed Tex Thornton, because her lover was her husband's father. I'll admit I didn't make that connection until late in the investigation, after I asked the most important question suggested by the A. D. Payne case. When investigative reporter A. B. MacDonald looked over the facts of the case, one fact stood out: The only person to benefit from Eva Payne's death was her husband. Who benefited from Randy Gorman's suicide? Paul Gorman and his wife, but I absolve Michele from any deliberate intent to drive her son to suicide. Her crime was being stupid and snobbish and controlling. If she had known her son's character at all—and she apparently didn't—she would have predicted that learning his father had been his wife's lover would have been a betrayal that he couldn't live with. That's what he meant when he told his brother, Jimmy, that "everything's gone that I believed in." Not only had the memory of his beautiful wife been tainted beyond bearing, but his own father was the one who besmirched his wife. Then his older brother and his cousin, two men who should have been his friends and confidants, attack him not only verbally but physically for being selected over them for an important position at Gorman Oil."

Bruce Gorman stirred. "I signed his death warrant, didn't I, when I appointed him manager instead of Paul?"

Megan evaded his eyes. "There was no way for you to know the consequences, Mr. Gorman."

"I suppose not, but that knowledge will not let me sleep any easier. And call me Bruce. I've lost any false pride that let me hold myself out as being better than you."

"You couldn't know what was going to happen, Mr. Gorman," said Lieutenant Roberts. "I was a cop, had been a cop for nearly thirty years, but I didn't make the connection of murder for gain. I just couldn't see a man killing his own son. So, if you want to blame yourself for Randy's suicide, you better blame me, too, 'cause I sure missed what an evil man your son was."

"I don't think either one of you can blame yourselves too much," said Candi Hobbs. "Paul Gorman was a sociopath, and most sociopaths are excellent at imitating normal emotions and behavior. I don't know how you could have known."

"Everyone hush. We can apportion blame after Megan is finished with her explanation," said Rosemary.

"Yes, tell us how the Boyce-Sneed feud resembled the Gorman case," asked Herb Jackson. I noticed he was making notes, so I suppose he would be spicing up his legal thriller with some of Megan's conclusions. Poor Herb. His book already had every kind of plot known to the mystery world. One more couldn't make it much worse.

"I think the similarities between the Gorman case and the Boyce-Sneed feud are the most striking," said Megan, holding out her cup to Agnes, who was pouring coffee. "We have two men in love with the same woman, but in this case, the men are not related. Paul, like Beal Sneed, is humiliated when his lover rejects him for a younger, more handsome man. Unlike Beal Sneed, Paul's fury is directed at the woman in the romantic triangle because first, Paul is married; and second, Randy is his son. If Melinda ever believed that Paul would divorce Michele, his socially acceptable wife, to marry her, she did not believe it long. Otherwise, I think she would have stayed with him, but as soon as Randy went to work at Gorman Oil, Melinda was making up to him. In other words, like Beal Sneed's neglecting Lena by traveling so much, Paul neglected Melinda by not marrying her. Both Lena and Melinda found some-one else. But as Beal Sneed refused to give up Lena, so Paul refused to give up Melinda. If he could not have her, then no one could, and the only way to keep her, the only way to keep from facing his humiliation each time he visited his son, was to murder Melinda."

Exhausted, she leaned back. "Paul and Michele were the last to talk to Randy before he began to pace up and down the hall, his stress building toward suicide. Paul is the only man whose betrayal Randy would not be able to live with. Imagine your own father sleeping with your wife, then letting you take the blame for her murder."

"What about the scorecards?" asked Rosemary.

"I think they showed that Michele was nervous be-yond bearing," replied Megan. "The question is: what could have made her so nervous? The knowledge that her husband's mistress was now her daughter-in-law? Or did she know that her husband planned to talk to Mel-inda? Did she see him walk across the lawn to the ga-zebo during one of the times she was dummy? When Randy found Melinda murdered, did she suspect her husband, and was caught between loyalties? Did Paul persuade her to keep silent, that Randy would never be convicted? I don't know. We may never know. But she stopped overbidding her hand at about the time the autopsy report said Melinda died."

"What a horrible woman!" exclaimed Candi.

Megan rubbed her forehead. "Have Lieutenant Roberts tell you about mama guppies sometime."

"You and Ryan and Herb did such a masterful job unraveling the case," said Agnes.

"It was mostly Megan," I said, not wanting to be cast as an amateur sleuth. "Isn't that right, Herb?"

"Absolutely," agreed Herb.

"And it was all psychological," said Agnes. "Remember what Hercule Poirot said at the end of *Cards on the Table?* "With the eyes of the mind one can see more than with eyes of the body." And that's what you did, Megan. You saw with the eyes of the mind."

"What did Paul yell out before he died, Megan?" said Randal. "I couldn't understand him."

I saw Megan exchange glances with Lieutenant Roberts, and I knew whatever she was going to say wouldn't be the truth. Whatever happened in that gazebo was a secret between Megan and Roberts, and I didn't expect either one of them to ever disclose it.

"I think he was hallucinating. He thought I was Melinda. And his death was fitting. A massive cerebral hemorrhage equates to having one's skull fractured with a pool cue."

EARLENE FOWLER

introduces Benni Harper, curator of San Celina's folk art museum and amateur sleuth

□ **FOOL'S PUZZLE**   0-425-14545-X/$5.99

Ex-cowgirl Benni Harper moved to San Celina, California, to begin a new career as curator of the town's folk art museum. But when one of the museum's first quilt exhibit artists is found dead, Benni must piece together a pattern of family secrets and small-town lies to catch the killer.

□ **IRISH CHAIN**   0-425-15137-9/$6.50

When Brady O'Hara and his former girlfriend are murdered at the San Celina Senior Citizen's Prom, Benni believes it's more than mere jealousy—and she risks everything to unveil the conspiracy O'Hara had been hiding for fifty years.

□ **KANSAS TROUBLES**   0-425-15696-6/$6.50

After their wedding, Benni and Gabe visit his hometown near Wichita. There Benni meets Tyler Brown: aspiring country singer, gifted quilter, and former Amish wife. But when Tyler is murdered and the case comes between Gabe and her, Benni learns that her marriage is much like the Kansas weather: bound to be stormy.

□ **GOOSE IN THE POND**   0-425-16239-7/$6.50
□ **DOVE IN THE WINDOW**   0-425-16894-8/$6.50